Black Diamond 2: Nicety

Black Diamond 2: Nicety

Brittani Williams

www.urbanbooks.net

Urban Books, LLC
78 East Industry Court
Deer Park, NY 11729

Black Diamond 2: Nicety ©copyright 2010 Brittani Williams

ISBN 13: 978-1-60162-270-9
ISBN 10: 1-60162-270-8

First Trade Paperback Printing May 2010
Printed in the United States of America

10 9 8 7 6 5 4

Distributed by Kensington Publishing Corp.
Submit Wholesale Orders to:
Kensington Publishing Corp.
C/O Penguin Group (USA) Inc.
Attention: Order Processing
405 Murray Hill Parkway
East Rutherford, NJ 07073-2316
Phone: 1-800-526-0275
Fax: 1-800-227-9604

Acknowledgments

I did it again, book number four! I thank God, for helping me through it because it was a rough process this time. Through illness I struggled and managed to get it done. I dedicate all that I do to my son as always because everything I do is for him.

Thanks mom and dad for always having my back and spreading the word about my work. I love you more than you know.

Thanks to all of my family and friends, you all mean a lot to me and I am blessed to have you all in my life.

My cousin Frances, you have been there so much for me over the past year and I greatly appreciate it. I am blessed to have such a kind-hearted person in my life. I love you.

To my friends Jennifer and Nikki, you both have been such good friends and I'm very glad that you are part of my life. Jen thanks for always checking in on me and Nikki thanks for just being there to talk, hang out with, and of course keep my hair tight! I love you both.

Big Lil, thanks for coming in and being my savior for the new business. Things were looking grim but you stepped in and made things look a little brighter.

To people like Ameer of UrbanSteez.com, Rell of the 1800Magazine.com, the *Dedan Tolbert Show*, Kenyatta of *Love & Life Magazine*, and all other magazines and book clubs. Your support hasn't gone unnoticed.

All of my author friends Anna J., K'wan, Mark Anthony,

Acknowledgments

Dashawn Taylor, Daaimah S. Poole, Karen E. Quinnones Miller, Nyema Taylor, J.M. Benjamin, Shay, T. Styles, K.D. Harris, Anya Nicole, and so many others, thanks for always being a positive influence and I hope you all continue to flourish in your careers. Each of you are an inspiration to me.

Neesh, thanks for taking that lead role of *Diamond* on for the stage play and for becoming a friend. I wish you so much success in your career. Ms. Cat, I'm so glad you hung in there with me, you are the bomb and I know your modeling and acting career will only continue flourish.

Tiona Brown, I want to congratulate you on your book and I'm glad that we've met and become friends. I look forward to your success as an author.

Thanks to Ralph, Ebey, Al, Babyman, Marv, Uncle Howie, and Buck Wild for the support. You have all supported me in some fashion and it means a lot. Thanks for promoting my work and me.

To everyone who has ever e-mailed me, went online and left a review, or stopped me to let me know how much you loved my books, thank you! Your support definitely keeps me going.

To anyone that I have forgotten, I sincerely apologize. It definitely doesn't mean you aren't important and I will make it up to you.

Ms. Brittani

Prologue

I hope you enjoyed the last two months—get ready for a war. You should have checked my pulse to see if I was dead. I couldn't believe my eyes nor could I believe such a thing was possible. Checked his pulse? Why hadn't I done that? I stood there in the office with both Kiki and Black staring me down, waiting for me to tell them what the letter said. I had detached myself from the situation. I had instantly flashed back to that night and tried to figure out what I'd missed. Black went inside after me so he should have noticed. Did he see what I saw? I never really wanted to talk about it after that night but I just couldn't understand how I'd been so careless. Yes, I was emotional, but this could be the end for me; this could be the end for both Black and me.

"Don't worry, you'll take care of it?" I yelled.

'That's what I said, don't worry about it."

"How the hell do you expect me to do that? There's no way I can act like I didn't just read that fucking note. How the hell could this happen, Black? What the hell are we going to do?"

Kiki stood still as a statue; she couldn't believe it either. She warned me about this, telling me that I needed to be careful and now look what happened. I wanted her to say something. I wanted someone to say anything that made sense at this point, because saying *don't worry* just wasn't going to get it. It just wasn't possible at a time like this.

"Didn't you see him, Black? What did you see when you went inside the house?"

"Diamond, I just told you what happened."

"Well, I need you to tell me again. Please tell me anything that would make this seem like a joke. This has to be a joke."

"I was sitting in the car when I saw you come out—I didn't see anyone else around. No cars or anything. I was sitting there waiting for Kemp to call me—we were supposed to go make a drop. I didn't know what the fuck was going on but I knew that something wasn't right. I waited until you pulled off and used the spare key Kemp gave me to go inside. I called his name and when I didn't get a response, I went upstairs and saw him lay out on the floor near the bed. I noticed that you tried to throw some things around but it looked staged so I hurried and ransacked the place a little more and then I left."

"He was on the floor?" I asked. From what I remembered he was on the bed, so how the hell did he get on the floor?

"Yeah, he was on the floor. Why does that matter?"

"Because when I shot him he was on the bed. How the hell could he have gotten on the floor unless he wasn't dead?"

Black stood there with a puzzled look on his face. I was still trying to figure this out, there had to be something that we were missing. Kiki still stood in the same spot, silent.

"He has to be dead, Diamond, it just doesn't make any sense."

"I know that it doesn't make sense but I know that someone knows something if they're sending shit like this."

"There was no one else there, though; I sat outside and didn't see anyone else."

"The note clearly says something different." I was frustrated. This was something that I didn't need to deal with—I couldn't deal with it.

"D, I'm kind of thinking Black's right. I mean, if he went in and saw him dead then it can't be him," Kiki finally chimed in, though she wasn't saying anything that I wanted to hear.

This situation had me questioning everyone and everything. I wanted this to be over, I wanted to believe that everything was going to be okay but it didn't appear that way. I took the note from Black's hand and read it again—I still couldn't believe my eyes. I grabbed my bag off of the chair and headed toward the door without saying a word. I heard footsteps behind me but I didn't turn to look.

"Diamond, wait," Black yelled.

"What, Black? I need to get home right now so talk to me when you get there."

"Why are you angry at me? I'm not the one that's doing anything. Shit, you shot him—I just tried to help you cover it up."

I turned around and gave him the stare of death. "I didn't ask for your fucking help, I didn't ask you for anything."

"I didn't mean it like that, Diamond. I'm just trying to figure out why you're mad at me."

"I'm not mad at you, I'm mad at myself. I fucked up and now I could be killed. Look, I have to go. I'll talk to you at home."

"I'm going to follow you, so just wait a minute. I don't feel comfortable with you traveling alone."

I didn't respond. I got in the car and drove off, leaving him standing there. I didn't want to be followed. I didn't want to feel like a damn criminal or a child. I wanted shit to be normal. I looked in the rearview mirror and didn't see him. I needed some time alone. There wasn't anything that he could say to make me feel better. The only thing that would make me feel better knowing Kemp's body was six feet under where I watched them lower it.

Chapter 1

Diamond

Tricks of the Trade, November 2007

I had to see for myself. If I had the strength to dig six feet under I would have brought a shovel out here to this cemetery. It was cold and dark. Most people would think I was crazy for coming out here alone at 12 A.M. but for once in my life I could honestly admit that I was afraid. I had done too much to turn back or to even apologize, for that matter. How could you say I'm sorry for shooting you? The fact of the matter was that I wasn't sorry for shooting him, I was sorry that he hadn't died. I was confused—I could remember that day as if it were yesterday. I stood there at the foot of the bed as both Kemp and Mica's blood poured out onto the sheets and soaked into the bed. Someone was trying to scare me and it was definitely working. He couldn't be alive. I didn't stay around to check his pulse but I knew it had to be him buried there. I put on an Oscar-worthy performance at the funeral, even kissed his cold cheek. I was sure that I had gotten away with murder. What was I supposed to do now? I got down on my knees and put my hand on the headstone that read his name. So many things were running through my mind at this point. I wanted to pray but then I'd feel guilty for what I'd done to get me in this position in the first place. In my mind, things like this only happened in the movies, people who were assumed dead would return to cause a ruckus, but not in the real world. I was losing my mind—I had to know one way or another who the hell was screwing with me. Someone else must've been there that night—that was the only explanation that I could come up with. I heard leaves breaking as if someone were stepping on them and breaking them into pieces. I quickly turned my head and looked around. I didn't see anyone. *What the hell was going on?* I thought.

"Who's there?" I spoke loudly enough to be heard, but not too loud to wake up the neighborhood. I wasn't trying to bring more attention to myself. The cemetery on Lehigh Avenue was directly across from residential homes so I knew if I got too loud they could hear me. Then I thought, maybe that was a good thing, in case someone was trying to attack me. "Who's there?" I spoke again but still no answer. I focused my attention back on the headstone but at the same time I reached in my purse and held onto my gun to be safe.

"I know that I buried you. I just don't get it. Who's down there?" I heard the leaves again. I was getting annoyed. I stood up from the ground and looked around again. "Who the hell is out here?" Still no one answered.

Maybe I was just being paranoid. It was mid-November and pretty windy out so it could have just been the wind blowing the leaves around. I looked at the headstone one last time before walking toward my car. I kept looking around the cemetery but with so many trees you could easily hide and not be seen. I still gripped onto my gun tightly, walking so fast I was practically running. The sound of the leaves breaking got louder the faster I walked. My cell phone rang just as I pressed the keypad to unlock the car doors and damn near gave me a heart attack.

"Hello," I said as I hurried inside of the car and locked the doors.

"Babe, where the hell are you?" Black yelled. I could tell that he was angry. With all of the stuff going on, he definitely didn't want me out of his sight. I ditched his security to come here. I couldn't stand to be followed.

"I'm on my way home. I'm just leaving the cemetery."

"The cemetery? What the hell would make you go to the cemetery at midnight? You need to get back here now."

"I just said I was on my way home." I knew he was worried but I wasn't a child. Hell, without me, he wouldn't have half of what he had now. He'd still be Kemp's understudy waiting for a chance to take the lead.

"Just hurry up!" he yelled into the receiver before hanging up. I didn't get a chance to respond but I was ready to curse him from A to Z. Shit, he should have learned from Kemp, no man was going to tell me what to do. Those days were long over. I started the car and tried to pull off but the car wouldn't move.

"What the hell?" I yelled. I got out and walked around to the back of the car and noticed both back tires were completely flat. Someone was definitely out here and the feeling of fear that came over my body damn near buckled my knees. I hurried back inside the car and dialed Black again.

"Come get me, somebody is out here trying to get me."

"What?"

"Black, just hurry up! Both of my back tires are flat and I heard someone following me. Please hurry up."

"I'm coming now."

I pulled my gun from my bag as I nervously sat and waited. I should have never been out there in the first place. Each time I saw movement I put my fingers in place to shoot. I laughed—when it would end up being a tree branch or a plastic bag flying in the air. Was I tripping? Or was there really someone out there? I kept asking myself over and over again until something came crashing through my back window. Glass went everywhere and I heard footsteps going in the opposite direction. Once I could clearly see, I yelled, "I have a gun and trust me, I'll shoot!" I was scared shitless and I prayed that Black would pull up at any minute. My prayers were answered when I saw the headlights of his BMW. I got out of the car and ran over almost, knocking him over.

"Someone is trying to kill me, they threw something through my back window. I'm so glad you came." I hugged him and held on tight. The river of tears began to flow once I knew I was safe. He walked me over to the passenger seat of his car and put me inside. He walked over to my car and looked at the tires and widows before making a phone call. I wasn't sure who he called and honestly, I didn't care. I wanted him to get inside of the car and take me the hell home. I'd had enough excitement for one night. He was still on the phone when he climbed into the driver's seat and drove off.

"All right, get with me and let me know what's up. I need Merk to tow that car early. I don't need that shit getting any extra attention . . . call me after he's done . . . I'm staying with her tonight and we'll link up tomorrow . . . all right one!" He turned and looked at me. I was still crying and shivering in my seat. He didn't say a word—he just reached over and put his hand on top of mine. I couldn't speak. I didn't know what to say. They say what goes around comes around and maybe it was my time to get what was coming for me. I walked into the house like a zombie. Black still didn't speak, which was probably a good thing because I didn't know what to say. I sat down on the couch and soon he sat down next to me.

"I'm glad you're okay," he finally broke the silence but I didn't respond. I looked over at him and kissed him. Shit, I was more than glad that I was okay. I should have never been so foolish in the first place. I couldn't figure out what the hell possessed me to go out to a damn cemetery at night anyhow. Though he was a man and he wouldn't be one if he didn't do or say the stupid shit that men do, he was the one that I loved. I mean, none of the other men in my past truly cared about me the way that Black did. With training, Kemp probably could have but Black didn't need any of that. He did it on his own. It was then that I appreciated him even more. He could have went out to work, which is what kept us living the lavish life but he chose to stay with me. We continued to kiss each other as if it were the last kiss we'd ever have. His hands were soon all over my body and my clothes had since hit the floor. His smooth skin next to mine felt like silk rubbing across my naked body. His movements were slow and deliberate and each touch hit spots that I didn't even realize could send chills up and down my spine. His body was sculpted to perfection and every muscle looked like chocolate greatness like it could melt in your mouth. I tried to relax and not exemplify how anxious I was but it was becoming more difficult to hold back with each second. His Sean John cologne was tickling my nose. I was in heaven waiting for him to reach my wet pussy and massage it as he'd done my nipples a few seconds earlier, but he chose to take his time. His hands slowly moved down my stomach and soon reached my throbbing clit, which was just about to erupt. My body began to shake on contact. The orgasm had been building up and just the slightest touch made me explode. Hell, he could have probably blown on it and gotten the same result.

I moved my hips to grind against his fingers as he continued to kiss me sensually. At that point, I wished that I hadn't waited so long to get with him. I mean, when I met Kemp, Black was hanging in his shadow. I was looking for a leader so naturally Kemp caught my attention. Since money was my main objective, being with Black back then wasn't an option. All I could see were dollar signs. I married Kemp just for the money but being with Black was totally different; it was for love. Kemp had never been a slacker in the lovemaking department but it was just something about Black that I couldn't explain. I had never been with a man who could look at me and cause my lips to quiver. He was perfect in every sense of the word and when I felt his thick fingers slide inside of me I began to fuck them. I moaned loudly but was soon silenced as his lips touched mine and his tongue quickly followed behind. He stared me in the eyes as if there was something that he wanted to say but couldn't find the words to speak. I wanted to know what was on his mind but I was enjoying the feeling of his fingers in my pussy too much to say a word.

"I love you," he whispered gently, almost like sweet poetry. With just the sound of those two words my body began to shake and my juices were running down his fingers and forming a puddle in the palm of his hand. I wanted to return the favor but he didn't allow me to. He got on his knees and slowly pushed his dick inside of me. He wasn't fucking me like he had any other time. He was making love to me and I was making love to him. I could lie in that position forever, with him inside of me.

"I love you more," I finally whispered back after a few minutes of his slow lovemaking. With a slow lick of his ear and the tightening of my pussy walls he erupted inside of me. His sweat was dripping all over my face and I didn't even budge to wipe it off. I let it dry into my skin. I wanted all of him, even the perspiration from our lovemaking. After lying next to each other quietly for a few minutes the thoughts of my earlier encounter crossed my mind. I didn't want to fuck up the mood but I had to know what was on his mind and what his plan was. Shit, I could have been killed so I had every reason to be nervous.

"What are we going to do, Black? I mean, if he's really alive we're as good as dead." I was still lying next to him with my head nestled in his chest. I could hear his heart beating and surprisingly it hadn't skipped a beat.

"I told you I would take care of it. Kemp doesn't scare me—he never has—but it can't be him, we both know that he's dead. I'm just focused on who the hell else knows what happened."

In a way I believed that what Black said was true, but hell, everyone was afraid of Kemp—or at least I thought that they were. Black was strong and it was one of the things that I loved most about him. I mean, who wanted to be with a wimp? Every woman wanted a man that could protect her. I wasn't crazy and I wanted to know who the culprit was just as much if not even more than Black.

"I know you told me Black, but we aren't together twenty-four hours a day. How can you protect me when you're not around? You saw what just happened."

"I know we're not together all the time but I have eyes everywhere. You have to trust me. I won't let anything happen to you. I've got you now and I'm not letting you go. You just can't put yourself out there like that again, babe. You have to work with me until I figure out what the hell is going on here."

Listen to him getting all sentimental, I thought. I smiled inside because for once I believed that it was true. I'd finally found a man that told me he loved me and meant it. Some would say that Kemp was in love with me and there were even some crazy people that would say Davey was too. I knew the truth and the fact of the matter is neither one of them really loved me. I was just something they could show off and be proud of. They could say they made me and yes, I admit it, they did make me. I didn't have shit before I met Davey and after my stint in prison I didn't have shit when I met Kemp either, so it wasn't a lie that I still wouldn't have shit if it weren't for them.

See, with Davey I was young and dumb. I fell for every word that he said and it didn't matter how many times he cheated or did me wrong, making up was always so good. He'd spoil me; he'd give me anything I wanted and I couldn't turn any of that away. I was living the good life—shit, much better than that raggedy-ass row home in North Philly. I had a huge apartment, a nice car, and a walk-in closet full of designer clothes and shoes. Yeah, it sounds foolish but when you come from my background you cling on to things that feel better even though there are bumps along the way. I remember feeling like there was no other man for me and begged Davey to stay when he'd threaten to leave. Because of all of the drama in my life, the nine months I spent in prison for Davey came to mind. That was the turning point in my life. Some would say that it wasn't in a good direction but I felt that it did. If you can emerge from a situation so devastating and come out on top it has to count for something. The days that I sat in my jail cell I had a lot of time to think. I thought about the time that he gave me a STD and defended the chick that he had locked in his bedroom, nearly choking me to death. I thought about the time that he talked me into having a threesome, which later ended up sold on DVD in the streets. If that wasn't bad enough, I learned that the woman I had sex with—for him, might I add—was the mother of his child—a child that I never knew he'd fathered. Then there was the straw that broke the camel's back, after doing a drop-off for him I was arrested when it turned out to be a setup. So there I was in the detention center serving time and he didn't bother to answer my calls, letters, send me a penny, or pay me a visit. It was almost as if he'd forgotten about me the day that they took me in. I was distraught. What the hell was I supposed to do? When I came home, I was broke as a bum on the corner. I had no place, no money, clothes or transportation. If it weren't for Kiki, I would have either landed in a shelter or back in North Philly with my hating-ass Aunt Cicely and all of her damn kids! I had to do something—something to survive. So any critic that thought I was wrong for searching out a man like Kemp in order to get to the top, could pucker up and kiss my ass because they weren't in my shoes to say what I should or shouldn't have done. But hey, if I wouldn't have met Kemp, I wouldn't have met Black and that's the wonderful thing—the thing that kept me smiling.

Black got off the sofa and I knew that it was time for work. Damn, I wanted to enjoy this moment. Being the head of an empire had its downfalls too. You never really get too much quality time. He walked upstairs to the bathroom as I lay there watering at the mouth. His body was a masterpiece. The muscles in his back were sculpted to perfection. His skin was smooth as melted chocolate and the sweat from our lovemaking gave his body just the right amount of shine. His ass was perfect too. I'd never seen an ass on a man like his. I just wanted to lie next to it all day long. Within a few seconds I heard the shower running and following that I smelled his Sean John body wash filling the air. I inhaled and got chills. I wanted to go meet him in the shower for round two but I knew he had to go to work. I rolled over and closed my eyes. I wasn't sleepy but my mind was exhausted. I knew that I would drive myself crazy trying to figure out how the hell I had gotten myself into this mess. I was so careful—well, at least I thought that I was. Black emerged from the bathroom about fifteen minutes later with a towel wrapped around his waist. By then I was sitting on the edge of the bed in the bedroom.

"Are you gonna be okay? If not, I'll get JB to send someone over here. Matter fact, I will have him do that anyway. I don't want to leave you here alone."

Though I wasn't really comfortable having the workers in

my house, it was the best thing to do. I knew that I wouldn't have been able to rest anyway, wondering if someone would creep in here while I was asleep and kill me. It may sound silly, but it was the truth—I was scared shitless.

"That's fine, I'd feel better with someone here anyway," I agreed. Black walked toward the closet and began to get dressed. I just sat there admiring him. I wondered how I'd gotten so lucky and found a man like him. I wished that I had found him a long time ago. Maybe then I wouldn't be sitting here fearing for my life. After he'd finished getting dressed he walked over to my side of the bed and kissed me good-bye.

I fell asleep and woke up around seven A.M. to a ringing cell phone. *Who the hell was calling me so early?* I fumbled through my bag lying on the bedside table to find it.

"Hello," I said in a low tone. I hadn't even fully opened my eyes yet. There were specks of light peeping in through the blinds, which nearly gave me a headache—probably from my lack of sleep.

"Babe, you won't believe this shit!" Black's loud voice woke me up instantly.

"What? What happened?" I was nervous. I didn't really want to hear the answer as I sat up in bed and fought with the sun to fully open my eyes.

"The fucking store on Hunting Park is burning down! I need to know what muthafucker had something to do with this. When I find his ass it's going to be a war for real."

"The store is burning down?" I couldn't believe it. I mean, it wasn't as if it was a big money spot but, shit, it did make money. What the hell were they trying to prove? This is definitely not what I wanted to wake up to. I knew things could only get worse from that point on. I was second-guessing my-self again. Who else but Kemp would have something to gain by terrorizing us? That night flashed in front of me like a film on television. I walked into my house as I did on any other day but when I pulled up in the driveway and noticed the car we'd let Mica use while she was working on getting back on her feet. It was strange because we hadn't seen each other in five years but in a few short weeks we'd become closer than we were before. In a way, I still felt bad about the fact that her brother murdered their father but I knew as well as she that I had no part of that. I loved her brother, and there was no way I'd want him to land in prison for the rest of his life. Maybe I shouldn't have trusted that our relationship could get back on track. Maybe I was a fool for thinking a woman couldn't possibly be interested in the person that murdered her man right in front of her. There I was, walking up the stairs with my heart beating a hundred beats a minute. I felt in my heart that something was wrong. Okay, yes, I planned to get rid of Kemp but I never thought I'd get betrayed by her.

As I made my way down the hall I could see the flickering of a candle and could hear the faint sounds of moaning. I walked slowly to avoid being heard. I almost burst when I saw her straddled on top of him. I instantly wanted to speak, yell, scream or do something other than what I was doing. I was standing there like a statue. My body was doing something totally different than my mind. In my mind I was moving in on them, letting my presence be known but my feet weren't budging. Instead, I stuck my hand into my bag and pulled out my handgun—a handgun that I carried for protection. This protective tool was now a weapon and before I knew it, blood was spraying all over the bed, walls, and pretty much every surface in the room. I didn't know what to do next. My first thought was to throw things around and make the house appear to have been robbed. I didn't bother to check and make sure they were both dead, all I could think about was getting out of the house without being seen. I hurried out of the house and returned just in enough time to find the police and ambulance scattered all around the driveway and lawn. I put on the performance of the grieving wife and was picked up by Kiki, who took me over to her apartment for the night. By the note and the recent incidents, I was sure someone knew what I'd done—but whom? But then, I was so disoriented I didn't even notice Black in his car watching me run into the car in a sweat suit carting a handful of trash bags. I could have missed someone else—hell, he could have missed someone else.

I was becoming angrier by the minute and the conversation with Black wasn't going that great either. I wanted to know what the hell was going on as I snapped back to reality.

"Yeah, I'll talk to you about it when I get home. I'm trying to wrap shit up with the cops now."

"Black—"

"I'll talk to you when I get home, I have to go."

Click!

I sat there and stared at the phone. I was tempted to call him back. I wanted to know what the hell was going on with my store. It just didn't make sense to me and Black's attitude wasn't making things any better. Yes, he ran the businesses but shit, I owned everything, so technically he worked for me. So the fact that he was being so brief was really pissing me off. I got up out of bed and rummaged through my closet for something to wear. I had to go down to the store and see it for myself. Black would be pissed but hell, I was pissed right now so he'd just have to deal with me being there. I put on a Juicy Couture sweat suit and headed out of the door. I still had to look the part since there'd probably be cameras and shit at the scene. I couldn't be caught slipping, not even on a bad day. I sped down to the store in the Mercedes-Benz Black bought me last month, which was a good thing since my Jaguar was sitting on two flats. I immediately noticed the yellow tape and police officers blocking off the scene. I could only get within a two-block radius. I parked and got out to walk over. Black smoke filled the air and you could see the three fire trucks pouring water onto the building. People were crowding around, trying to get a glimpse of the building. I heard a few old ladies talking as I walked by.

"There she goes, right there. I'm glad that fucking store is burning."

"Yes, keep the drugs off of our block!"

I didn't respond. I didn't even turn around to see who said what. It didn't matter. I knew how they felt—I felt that way once. I lived in a neighborhood full of drug dealers and crack-heads, and I hated it. So I'm sure people would wonder how I could grow up and fall into the same line of work. Well, the answer is pretty simple: money. Money was my motivation and after all that I'd been through there wasn't any other job out there for me. I saw Black, JB, and a few other workers in a huddle near the corner. I walked over.

"What are you doing here?" he yelled.

"I had to see the store for myself."

"You don't need to be here." He grabbed me by the arm so we could walk away from the workers.

"Yes, I do, Black, it's my store."

"Okay, now that you've seen it, you can go home."

"I'm not going anywhere."

"Why do you have to be so stubborn? Just go home and I'll take care of it."

I stood there silent. I wanted to believe that he could but I wasn't so sure looking at the building burning to the ground. Whoever it was definitely wasn't going to stop until we were both out of the picture. I wasn't going to stand out there in front of everyone and argue with him so I agreed to leave and quietly headed toward my car. I was angry. Not at Kemp or Black but at myself for letting this happen. I got in the car and looked around to see if I saw anyone suspicious. Who the hell was I looking for? For some reason, I still hoped I'd see Kemp. At least that way we'd know who to look for. I didn't really think they'd be stupid enough to hang around the scene but shit, that could be cockiness too. If it were Kemp, he knew we'd never turn him into the cops after what I'd done to him and Mica and if it wasn't him we wouldn't know where to start pointing the finger anyway. I was paranoid. I started the car to drive home. I had to clear my head. I couldn't live the rest of my life looking over my shoulders wondering when someone was going to kill me. I had to focus on something else so that I could move on with my life. Black wouldn't let anything happen to me. He promised me that and I had to believe him. I had to obtain that thug mentality that men have, the one that sheds all of the fear. I had to learn the tricks of the trade if I wanted to make it in this business.

Chapter 2

Black

Mind over Matter

"So what's the next move?" JB stared at me, waiting to hear something. I didn't know what the next move was. How can I know what to do to a nigga that's supposed to be dead? And then, what if it wasn't him after all? I'd be wasting time looking for him and someone else could catch me off guard. I wasn't trying to get caught slipping. I had to figure this shit out.

"Let's go to the house, I don't want to stand out here and talk," I replied before turning to walk toward the car. I honestly wanted some time to think. Being alone on the drive would hopefully help me decide what I was supposed to do next.

"Cool, meet you there in twenty minutes."

I got in my car and headed toward the safe house. I didn't even turn the music on. I was too deep in thought. I had to either figure out what their next move was or wait for them to slip up and reveal their identity. I knew Kemp like the back of my hand and with enough thought I knew I could figure him out. But an unknown assailant wouldn't be that easy. Shit was just going as planned. I had snagged the woman I wanted. Diamond was the perfect woman with the business and respect to go along with it. I was turning into the king that I worked hard to become. I'd be dammed if I was going to let a mutha-fucker come in and snatch it away from me. The ride seemed longer than normal since my mind was completely occupied. Everything was moving in slow motion. Diamond kept calling my cell but each time it rang, I sent it to voicemail. I couldn't talk to her right at that moment—shit, I didn't know what to say. I had promised her that I would protect her and now it didn't look like I could. She was always so dramatic so I knew that it would turn into a long, drawn-out episode and I wasn't in the mood for the soap opera shit right then.

JB, Tommy, and Kenyon were waiting outside when I pu-lled up at the safe house. Like three soldiers they stood wait-ing for orders. With three totally different personalities and all from different backgrounds, they made the perfect army. JB was from uptown, an only child whose only parent was the TV. Most times he'd steal from the corner stores to eat. His mother had been locked up for armed robbery since he was seven and at ten he moved in with his drug-addicted aunt. Getting high was her main concern so her children were forced to grow up long before their time. JB refused to go back to foster care so he struggled to keep things in order when the social workers would come to visit. He met Kemp when he was seventeen while trying to get into the drug game. Kemp noticed his potential and quickly took him under his wing. Tommy was from West Philly and what I'd call a loose cannon. Tommy came from a two-parent middle-class home but stayed in so much trouble he was put in the youth study center at fifteen. He was released after his eighteenth birthday right into the arms of Kemp. Tommy didn't know any other way to survive since he had a criminal record. The fast life grabbed ahold of him and hadn't let him go ever since.

Last there was Kenyon—the brains is what I'd call him. He was much smarter than the average nigga and that alone made him the deadliest of them all. A single mother who always showed him the importance of education raised him. Yes, in school he was the nigga with straight As, but if you picked a fight with him, instead of fighting you he'd come up with a plan for you to hurt yourself more than he ever could. He got drafted into the game because of that. See, most of the niggas in the game will shoot first and ask questions later. Fuckin' with Kenyon, you'd put the gun to your temple and blow your own fuckin' brains out. He could say the slickest shit to get in your head and have you second-guessing everything you'd ever learned. He threw me for a loop when I first met him because he always kicked that intellectual shit. I wondered how a nigga so smart could end up selling drugs. But the craziest part of it all is how he had just as much if not more money than Kemp and had never touched the drugs that got him there.

I parked and sat in the car for a few seconds before getting out. I wanted to build the suspense. I knew that they were wondering what I had planned.

"Yo', what's the deal, man? Who are we going to war with?" JB asked as soon as I stepped out of the car.

"Let's go inside," I responded, before walking toward the door.

We all walked inside the house. I was still silent. I knew as soon as I told them who I thought was doing everything they were going to go crazy. They'd never understand why, so I had to think hard on how I'd reveal my thoughts.

"So who burned down the store?" Tommy asked, while taking a seat at the kitchen table.

I stood there and stared at them. They all stared back, waiting to hear my response. They were like children in a classroom waiting to be taught. "Kemp," I answered in a low tone, hoping that they wouldn't hear me.

"Kemp? What the hell do you mean? He's dead!" Kenyon yelled immediately. I knew what reaction I was going to get from him. He was the type that didn't believe shit stunk unless you put it right under his nose.

"Yeah, that's what I thought too but we got this strange note that points to him and now this shit with Diamond and the store. In my heart, I know he's dead but the note makes me question that," I replied, hoping that I wouldn't have to go any further.

"What note? What did it say?" Tommy stood up and stared at me, probably wondering why I hadn't revealed the note sooner.

"There was a note sent to the office saying that he hoped Diamond enjoyed the past few months." I conveniently left out the part about checking his pulse. I wasn't ready to reveal the fact that Diamond had shot him. I didn't know how they would react if they'd found out and I didn't want to take that chance. They had all grown to respect her as their boss, but they would most likely feel betrayed if they knew the true facts of that night. How could they trust the person that robbed them of not only their leader but their friend? If it weren't for me, they would have probably all went separate ways, but

I convinced them to stay on board. To find out what she'd done and then to know that I knew and did nothing about it, would only make things worse. I couldn't risk it. Especially when I didn't know who was out to get us. Every time I convinced myself it couldn't be him something inside made me think it was. The letter, to me, meant that someone was there and knew what went down. I didn't believe it myself at first and I probably wouldn't know if I hadn't seen it with my own eyes.

"What the hell does that mean? Why would he say some shit like? It doesn't make sense. We all know Kemp's dead, man—I was there. Why do you think it's him when you were right there with me? " Tommy asked with a puzzled look on his face.

"That can't be it and there has to be something that you're not telling us. Nothing you just said makes sense." Kenyon was seeing right through me but I had to keep it cool. I wasn't about to tell them the truth no matter how hard they pushed.

"I don't know what it is, Kenyon, all I know is someone is trying to take me and her under. I can't let that shit go down like that."

They all sat quiet and confused. If it were Kemp, how was I supposed to convince them to go to war with the man that helped them all get to where they were today? In reality, Kemp had helped us all. I waited for one of them to speak but they didn't. I didn't know what else to say. What I did know was that I wasn't going down without a fight and I damn sure wasn't going to let anyone hurt Diamond.

"So what are we going to do?" JB broke the five-minute silence that followed my last reply. Both Kenyon and Tommy

turned to look at him with the stare of death. They had definitely always been loyal to Kemp and with just the thought
of him being alive they were stuck between a rock and a hard
place. Would they remain loyal to him or me, the nigga that
was currently keeping their pockets fat if it turned out to be
Kemp?

"What the fuck do you mean *we*? Nigga, I'm not doing shit
until I know who the fuck I'm fighting. If it's Kemp, why
the hell should I be fighting? His beef ain't wit' me," Tommy
blurted out loud as he stood up from the chair that he was sitting in. JB stood up as well and was now standing face-to-face
with Kenyon.

"So you just gonna bail out on Black after all the shit he's
done? That's some sucka shit."

"Man, fuck you, I'm far from a sucka," he yelled back at JB,
pointing in his face. I could see where things were heading
so I stepped in the middle to try and calm them both down.

"Look, I know where you're coming from and I don't expect you to go to war with Kemp, but I gotta do what I gotta
do. I'm not gonna just lay down and get killed," I said after
they both sat back down. "Do what you have to, man, all of
you, and I'll do the same." I turned my back and headed toward the door. As I was climbing into the car JB ran out to
stop me.

"Yo' Black!" he yelled before reaching the rear of the car.

"What's up?"

"I'm wit' you all the way, I just want you to know that I got
your back."

"I appreciate that, man, and I'll get up with you later. I
have to go check on D." I reached out and gave him dap be-

fore getting into the car. He stood there facing me. I noticed Kenyon and Tommy standing at the door, watching. Now, not only did I have to worry about Kemp or some unknown killer, I had to worry about them too. Their loyalty was definitely to him and that wouldn't change. Even though they were working for me, to them, if Kemp were here I'd still be a worker just like them. Thinking back, I'd always been loyal to Kemp even if it got me caught up. One situation in particular showed just how loyal I was. It was 1995 and I had just gotten my first car. Shit, I was so happy you couldn't smack the smile off my face. It was a dark blue Acura Integra. I thought I was the shit! I was driving through all of the neighborhoods where the chicks were slower than the speed limit just to be seen. I had my Jay-Z, *Reasonable Doubt*, CD blasting as I bobbed my head with one hand on the steering wheel. Of course I'd purchased it courtesy of drug money. I hadn't been in the game very long but I vowed to purchase myself a car as soon as I got enough money to afford one. Kemp and Kenyon were standing on the corner in front of Papi's, the Puerto Rican store that we would get all of our candy and whatever else we needed. I pulled up slowly and rolled down the window.

"What's up, niggas?" I said loudly to make sure that I gained their attention. Kemp had his back turned but eased off of the car he was sitting on when he heard my voice. He was now facing me with a big smile on his face.

"I see you couldn't wait to spend that money, nigga. I like it. You trying to be a mini-version of me or something?" He burst into laughter. Kenyon joined in.

"Come on now, you know damn well I ain't tryna be you. You got too many hos with contracts on you." I grinned and pointed at him as he stood there laughing but underneath you could tell the comment rubbed him the wrong way. He definitely didn't find that funny. He'd screwed so many women over, one of them was bound to shoot his ass one of these days, I thought. I put on the hazard lights and opened the door to get out of the car. I couldn't believe it myself. Shit, I looked cleaner than the board of health riding around in that car. Kemp walked over and gave me dap as Kenyon followed up.

"This shit clean, nigga, you lucky I like you 'cause I'd jack your ass for this one," Kemp laughed.

"Yo' Kenyon, I'ma take a ride with him. I gotta holler at him about something. Meet me at the crib around six."

"All right," he replied before Kemp motioned for me to get back in the car. I didn't know what the hell he had to talk to me about but the look on his face told me that whatever it was he was going to make me listen—whether I wanted to or not.

Kemp got in the car and looked around without speaking. I did the same while I waited to see what it was he had to say.

"So what's the deal?" I asked, finally breaking the silence. He turned to look at me with a stare that said if looks could kill I'd be dead.

"You need to take this car back"

"Take it back? Why?" I was instantly pissed. I definitely respected Kemp and was appreciative for all that he'd done but he wasn't my father.

"It'll get too much attention."

"You're driving around in a BMW so why is that any different?"

"Because you gotta crawl before you walk. Shit, last week

your ass was on the bus—now you got an Acura. If you want to have longevity in this game you have to use your head. I'm successful because I'm smart and you can be too if you play your cards right."

"So where are we going?" I asked changing the subject.

"Yo', did you hear what I just said?" His tone changed from one of concern to one of anger.

"Yeah, man, I heard you. I'll take it back and get something else." I was pissed but without this game I wouldn't be able to afford it anyway. I already knew that there wasn't any negotiating with him. Once his mind was made up there wasn't anything that could change it.

"Pull over!" he yelled. I wasn't even at a complete stop before he jumped out of the car, pulled out his gun, and ran over to a group of guys on the corner. A few of them scattered immediately. Two men remained and stood frozen. I jumped out the car and pulled out my gun just in case something popped off.

"Where's my money, nigga?" Kemp yelled with the gun against the man's chin. The man's name was Jojo. Jojo was a local Jamaican hustler who purchased weight from Kemp. Leading up to that day, Jojo hadn't been paying up, claiming that there had been a recent drop in sales. It was a bullshit story because one of his workers had recently told Kemp all about what he did with his money. The informant told Kemp how Jojo would take the product that he got on consignment, cut it in half—lowering the purity—and then doubled the price. He was making damn near triple what he'd have to pay Kemp for the original product. After Kemp heard about it, he stopped letting him get any more cocaine until he paid the back money he owed. Three months had passed since the last payment and this particular day was the first time he'd seen him since.

"I don't have it yet, man. Shit is still slow around here," Jojo replied while the other man stood still as a statue.

"Do you think I'm a fool? I'll shoot your ass dead right where you stand. Don't fuck with me, where's the money?" He started patting him down while still holding the gun just under his chin. He retrieved a wad of money from one of his pockets. "What do we have here? Looks like money to me, muthafucker," he yelled before hitting Jojo on the side of the head with the gun. Blood instantly poured from his temple. Some of the excess splashed onto Kemp's fresh white T-shirt.

"I'm sorry, man, I need that money to feed my family. I promise I'll pay up. Just give me another week."

"Feeding your family sounds like a personal problem. Nigga, you owe me. I'm going to take this as a down payment now but I want the rest of my money by Friday." He moved closer to Jojo and forced part of the gun up his nose. Jojo was damn near crying as his friend still stood behind him, not saying a word. "And if I don't have my money, next time your head won't be the only thing bleeding."

Kemp backed away toward the car. I knew that was my cue. I jumped into the car and drove off as soon as Kemp sat down. He sat unfolding and counting the money that he had just taken from Jojo.

"That muthafucker messed up my damn shirt," he said as he looked down, noticing the spattered blood pattern on the front of his shirt.

"You want me to drop you off at home?"

"Yeah, I told Kenyon to meet me at the spot at six so I still got a little time. I can probably sneak in a quickie or something while I'm at it." He laughed. I joined in the laughter. "But back to you, man, I need you to take this car back and get a Honda or something. This car is going to get you too much attention way too fast. Don't get ahead of yourself, you might fuck around and end up like that nigga Jojo back there."

I nodded, agreeing. I respected him and he'd been in the game much longer than me so he was definitely wiser. I followed his order and the following day, I went back to the dealership and took the Acura back. I drove off the lot in a used Honda Accord. It was nowhere near as flashy and wouldn't get me much attention. At the time I didn't really understand why, but I never understood a lot of shit Kemp said or did. It was sort of like a teenager and their parents. They never understand why they have to obey them but later when it turns out to have been the best choice, they're thankful. That's how I felt but in that situation and many more that would come about in the future, mind over matter was how they worked. It was also a motto that got me where I was at that point. Being a boss took brains.

Chapter 3

Diamond

Fatherless

"Diamond! Hurry up and get down here for breakfast," my mother, yelled through the house. It was almost seven A.M. and the school bus would be there by seven-thirty. I hated waking up so early and I think my mother hated waking me up just as much. It was always a fight to get me out of the door on time. My dad was sitting at the table when I got there and as usual, him and my mom didn't have much to say to each other. Most days they sat across from each other without speaking a word. I walked to my father's side of the table and gave him a kiss on the cheek. For the first time since I was around five years old he didn't kiss me on my cheek as well.

"Is everything okay, Daddy?" I asked, still standing on the side of his chair. He set his newspaper down and looked me in the eye.

"Everything is fine, sweetie; Daddy's just got a lot on his mind, that's all." After his response he picked his paper back up off the table and resumed reading it. I knew that something wasn't right but I didn't want to ruin everyone's morning by probing him for more information. I slowly walked away and slid into my seat opposite his. There was a small bowl of oatmeal and a glass of milk sitting in front of me. The air in the room felt weird. I couldn't put a finger on what was different but I could feel it in the pit of my stomach. My mom was standing over the sink washing dishes as we continued to eat in silence. The date was October 13th and I remembered it because of a fire just a few blocks away. One of my best friends lived in that house and hadn't made it out alive. The date seemed significant to me at the time because of the loss, but by the end of that day I would not only lose my best friend but my father as well.

I had just scraped the last bit of oatmeal from the bowl and finished the glass of milk when I heard the school bus pulling up outside. I jumped up out of the chair and grabbed my book bag off of the floor. Just as I was about to head to the door my dad grabbed me by the arm and pulled me into a hug. The hug was much different than any other hugs because he wouldn't let go. I mean, he held onto me like it was the last hug that I would ever get. After he let go, I kissed him and walked out of the door. I glanced back before stepping onto the bus and noticed him standing at the door with a blank look on his face. That blank look was one that would haunt me for years since it was the last time that I'd see his face. I returned home that day and found out that he'd left us and wasn't coming back. I also learned that I was adopted. At first, I didn't know how to handle it. In school I was distant and my grades showed it. And if things couldn't get any worse, we lost our house because my mother couldn't pay the bills. We were forced to move in with my grandmom, in a raggedy row home in North Philly.

I hated living there. I was used to having my own room and my own things. There, I not only had to fight for my things I damn near had to fight for food. My cousins were bigger and much stronger than me so when it was time to eat I'd quickly be pushed aside and forced to eat the scraps that were left. Then my Aunt Cicely was the meanest bitch I'd ever known. Not a day went by where she wouldn't throw the fact that I wasn't really part of the family in my face. As if knowing it wasn't bad enough, I had to hear it every day. I would go to bed each night wondering why my real parents gave me away. From the day I found out, my mother tried her best to convince me of how special I was. I couldn't see it, since my biological father and the father that I'd always known not only left me but my real mother had as well.

Next there were the boys. I just couldn't get enough of them. I lost my virginity at the age of twelve and had sex with at least five boys by the time I met Johnny. Unlike the rest of them, Johnny couldn't care less about sex. I, on the other hand, was addicted. I loved the feeling of being wanted. The attention that they gave me somehow filled the void that my father had left me with. When one would leave, I'd quickly find another one to replace him. This cycle was one of the most reckless I'd taken part in my whole life.

The first time Johnny and I had sex, it was almost like I was a teacher and he was the student. Johnny, Mica, and me were watching TV in their basement. It was cold outside and not much heat was circulating. We were covered up with fleece blankets all piled up next to each other on the sofa. Mica had fallen asleep halfway into the movie and both Johnny and me were wide awake. Hidden underneath the blanket, my hand was rubbing his knee. Soon it was up to his thigh and next I was caressing his package, which was tightly nestled in his underwear. For once, he didn't stop me and since he hadn't, I took full advantage of the situation. He leaned over and began kissing me while palming my overdeveloped breasts at the same time. By now, I was unzipping his pants and sliding my hand into the opening. I could tell he was excited as his dick grew three more inches than normal. I prayed that he wouldn't stop me as he'd done the few times we'd made it this far. Mica was still sleeping, snoring loudly with drool slowly sliding down the side of her face. We were kissing and tonguing each other down so heavily that you could hear the smacking even over the TV. I stopped him just long enough to ease down on the floor. I motioned with my finger for him to join me. He obliged and within seconds we picked up where we had left off. Instead of getting completely naked I removed just my shorts. Johnny had his pants and underwear pulled down to his knee. I lay on my back as he crawled on top of me and struggled to find my warm opening. With one hand I grabbed hold of his dick and guided it inside of me. He let out a sigh immediately. I knew that he'd never had sex before so I didn't expect him to go very long. Surprisingly, he got into a rhythm and was still going fifteen minutes later. I guess some men are just born with it because for it to have been his first time he lasted longer than most of the boys I had been with. About twenty minutes later he was shaking and moaning on top of me. I covered his mouth with my hand to muffle the sounds that were escaping. After we were done, I hurried into the bathroom to wipe myself off and got

back in position at the far end of the sofa. Johnny looked over
at me and quietly said, "I love you" before focusing his attention back on the movie. I never wanted to tell Mica about our
first time. I figured she'd be mad that we did it while she slept
a few feet away.

Eventually, I had to tell her and everyone else when I found
out that I was pregnant. My mother was pissed. I didn't understand how I'd managed to sleep with five boys, numerous
times each and hadn't gotten pregnant. I was practically shaking when I told her that I had missed my period. She sat across
from me, quiet, while continuing to smoke her cigarette.

"So you missed your period? I guess that wouldn't mean
anything unless you were out there screwing. Is that what
you're telling me? You've been out there fucking those little
boys?" I was silent, afraid to look her in the eye. I was afraid of
seeing the disappointment. What mother would be proud of
her teenage daughter carrying a baby? "I don't hear anything.
I just asked you a question." Her voice was louder than it had
been a few seconds ago, which to me showed fury.

"I'm sorry, Mom, I didn't think I could get pregnant."

"Why not? Don't you learn that shit in school? As soon as
you get a period you can get pregnant. I'm so disappointed in
you, Diamond. I expected so much more from you."

Hell, I expected more from me. I also expected that I'd
always have a father around that loved me, but obviously that
wasn't the case. I didn't know what to say or do. I did know
that I wasn't ready to take care of a baby.

"I'm not ready to take care of a baby, Mom."

"Who said anything about taking care of a baby? I'm taking
you to the clinic first thing Monday morning to get rid of it.
I'll be damned if you're going to embarrass me."

I sat there with tears forming in the wells of my eyes. I was scared. I didn't think she would force me to get an abortion. I thought we could probably give it up for adoption. I knew my mother very well and what she said was pretty much what happened. There wasn't anything that I could do to make her think any different. Then I thought about it a little more. It was the right decision for all of us. Johnny definitely didn't want me to have the baby. He felt that it would ruin both of us and he probably was right. That Monday morning when she dragged me down to the clinic in the frigid weather, all I could think about was getting my life back to normal as quickly as possible.

The clinic was packed and most of the girls there were around my age. I guess I wasn't the only one dumb enough to think I couldn't get knocked up. After filling out all of the paperwork, we sat in the waiting room for hours. It was almost noon when they finally called my name and we'd been there since seven-thirty in the morning. They led me down a long hallway that had bright white paint like you see on TV. My mother stayed out in the waiting area with the other mothers and young girls waiting for their turn.

The nurse took me into a small room that had two changing stalls and a bathroom. She handed me a clear bag that contained a hospital gown, socks, and a cap for your head. She instructed me to take everything off, put on the things in the bag, and fill it with all of my belongings. I could barely get my pants unbuttoned I was so nervous. I didn't know what was about to happen to me. They hadn't explained it to me, only saying that my mother wouldn't sign for me to be put under anesthesia. Was that a form of punishment? How could she force me to be wide awake when they ripped my baby from the womb? I almost thought about running out of there and hitchhiking a ride home. The nurse startled me when she returned and reached out for my bag of belongings.

"Come with me. I'll put your things in a locker. I'm going to take you into the procedure room and prep you. Do you have any questions for me?"

"Is it going to be really painful?" I was scared shitless, still unaware of what was about to take place. I mean, I knew that I was going to leave here not pregnant anymore but I didn't know what would happen between now and then.

"It will be a little painful but doing it without anesthesia is the best way to do it. You won't feel groggy or possibly have any bad after-effects. Don't worry, I'll be in there with you the whole time. You can hold on to me and squeeze my hand if you need to."

I felt a little better after that but I was still a little uneasy. The procedure room was freezing cold. There was a table in the center surrounded by a bunch of machines. I assumed that most of them were to monitor your vital signs and things of that nature. Just from TV shows and things I saw in school, I saw the resemblance. I lay down on the table and tried to relax as I placed my feet in the stirrups and scooted down to the edge of it.

The doctor entered the room a few minutes later in a blue gown and gloves.

"This will be over before you know it. Scoot down a little more for me."

I was so uncomfortable. A grown man who was a complete stranger had his face down in my young pussy. I had never even been to a gynecologist before so this was all new to me. I followed his instruction and slid down so that my butt was at the end of the table.

"Okay, now you'll feel some cold fluid. I'm cleaning the area. Now a little pinch."

I damn near jumped off the table. A little pinch, my ass. Whatever he had just done hurt like hell. "Okay just a few more pinches." I held in the screams as he continued to stick needles in me. Tears were rolling down the sides of my face and landing on the paper that covered the table beneath me. Next came a loud machine and then I heard what sounded like a vacuum. My stomach was cramping beyond belief. Not even my worse day of PMS felt that bad. After a few more minutes of cramping, the loud machine stopped and the ex- perience was over. I was so weak that I could barely stand when the nurse helped me off of the table and into a wheel- chair. I recovered for about an hour before I was allowed to get dressed and meet my mother outside. Once she saw me, she walked around to the driver's side of the car and got in. The ride home was completely silent. She hadn't even asked how I felt. I guess she didn't care since I'd gotten myself into the situation in the first place. I didn't even have the ener- gy to try and spark up a conversation because she probably wouldn't have joined in anyway.

Following the abortion, Johnny was afraid to touch me. Honestly, I wasn't so anxious to have sex either. I'd be damned if I'd go through that shit again. Things between us remained the same and I was extremely happy that they did. I'd be lost without his love or the love of any man for that matter. Being fatherless screwed me up and pretty much set the tone for the way I'd search for a replacement. Of course I'd never find a man who would love me the way that he did, but at least I could dream about it.

Chapter 4

Black

Me and My Bitch

Besides Diamond, Trice was the only chick that knew how to make me come back for more. Shit, pussy was pussy but every once in a while you run across one that's exceptional. I wasn't ready to go home just yet. I was still trippin' about Kemp and if I'd gone home that's all Diamond would end up talking about. I needed to relax and what better way to do so than getting some bomb-ass head. I'd spoken to her earlier that day and told her I'd be by later that night so I knew she'd be ready. I parked, hit the alarm on the keypad, and headed to the door. Trice opened it wearing a pair of tight-ass shorts where her ass was hanging out of the bottom and a T-shirt that showed her hard nipples. She hadn't even pushed the door closed before I stuck my tongue in her mouth and grabbed hold of her ass. I was horny as hell and anytime I wanted sex with no strings attached, this was the place to be. Trice playfully pushed me away. I stared at her as she backed away.

"You've been a bad boy. I'm not really sure you deserve this pussy."

I smiled for the first time in a few days. She knew exactly

what I liked. I loved her playfulness especially when I needed a boost for the day.

"A bad boy, huh? Well, tell me how I can make it up to you because I definitely want the pussy." She moved closer to me as I now stood in front of the sofa. She gave me a push that forced me to sit down on the sofa. I sat looking up at her with a huge smile on my face. My dick was already damn near busting through my jeans. She slowly removed her T-shirt and shorts to revealed her naked body underneath. I wanted to grab hold of her and pull her on top of me but I didn't, I let her continue to lead.

"You see this? All of this is for you. Do you want it?"

"Of course I want it."

"How bad? I need you to make me believe it. If not, you won't even get to sniff it."

I let out a laugh. She was funny as hell but I knew that she meant it. As bad as she missed me, if I didn't convince her that I missed her just as much she wouldn't budge.

"More than ever, babe, I was thinking about you all day. Couldn't wait to get here."

"Oh, really, what were you thinking?"

"About those juicy-ass lips and that soft ass that I couldn't wait to touch."

She turned around so that her ass was facing me. "Go head and touch it."

I smiled and pulled her closer while rubbing my hands across her ass. It was soft as a baby's ass and I couldn't resist planting kisses all over it. She moaned and stuck it out a little further. I took one hand and massaged her clit from behind. Her juices were damn near pouring out. I couldn't wait to shove my dick inside of her. Her ass was still facing me as I stuck my finger inside of her. Within seconds her body began to tremble and the moans were even louder than before. I was afraid that she'd wake the kids, she was so damn loud.

"So that's how you feel?" she asked, smiling. I nodded but remained silent. She got down on her knees in front of me and loosened my belt before unzipping my pants and letting my dick breath. She put her lips on the head and planted a kiss that immediately made me sigh. She followed with one lick up the shaft and back down before deep-throating it, catching me off guard. That was damn near enough to make me bust right in her mouth. She smiled when she looked up and noticed the faces that I was making. I couldn't take anymore. I pulled her up from the floor, turned her around so that her back was facing me, and made her sit down on top of me. Her pussy was soaking wet as my dick made its way inside. I lifted up off the seat to meet her as she moved up and down on it. I knew I was about to disappoint her because it felt too good to do a marathon that night. I held onto her hips and my cum for all of ten minutes before I exploded inside of her. My body shook uncontrollably for a few seconds. That was just what I needed to relax. I sat there on the sofa with my head back after she went upstairs in the bathroom. She returned with a hot washcloth, which she placed on top of my dick, which forced me to open my eyes. I was about to grab hold of it until she began to wipe me off. Damn, I thought, if I didn't love Diamond as much as I did, she'd be mine again.

I fell asleep and hadn't even looked at the time before I did. I felt my cell phone vibrating and knew it was Diamond before I even picked up. I let out a little sigh before rolling out of bed and pressing talk on the phone.

"Hello?"

"Why haven't you answered any of my calls?"

"Because I was busy, Diamond, what's up?"

"What's up? Nigga, I've been calling you for three fucking hours."

"I said I was busy, what's up?"

"Somebody's been calling here, threatening me."

"Did you call JB?"

"Why would I call JB, you're my man, not him!"

"I'll be there in a little bit Diamond all right. I'm sorry, okay."

"Not as sorry as that bitch next to you will be if you don't answer my calls next time"

Click!

"Wifey's pissed, huh?"

"Yeah, I gotta go but I'll holla at you later." I leaned over and kissed her before getting up to get dressed. I didn't want to argue with Diamond but I knew that it was inevitable. I thought that going over to Trice's would keep me relaxed but the second I felt the vibration of the phone the relaxation was over. Things were great with Diamond and me up until this shit with Kemp started up. I mean, I could definitely under-stand her frustration but, shit, I was in it just as deep as she was. Not that I was scared of Kemp, but I'd known Kemp a lot longer than she had, which meant I knew what he was capable of. I always felt that I was stronger than him in many ways because for one, I knew how to keep my anger under control and two, he had more enemies than any nigga I knew. To him, that was power but to me it was foolish. Not that I wanted to be everyone's friend— that wasn't it by a long shot—

I just knew that when it was time to go to war it was better to have more niggas ready to fight with you then take your ass down.

I pulled up in front of the house and sat in there staring at the house. Kiki's car was in the driveway, which was never a good sign. See, Kiki was drama. Though she was Diamond's best and pretty much only friend she still got on my last nerve. At times she'd been the word of wisdom and I could appreciate that since Diamond normally didn't think before she made a dumb decision, but then there were times like these when I knew that she would only make things worse between her and me. I was hesitant going in but I had to make sure that things were under control. I knew that she was afraid and deep down I was afraid too. Not of what could potentially happen to me but what could happen to her. Regardless of the ups and downs, I cared about Diamond more than I'd cared about any woman. It just pissed me off when she didn't believe that I would do whatever I had to, to protect her.

Entering the house I could hear Kiki's ranting about me. I could hear Diamond, in a low voice, telling her to hush. I almost turned back around and left but I wanted to look her in the eye with a stare so she'd know I'd heard what she'd said. When I walked into the living room, she rolled her eyes and turned to hug Diamond before getting up and heading toward the door. I stood there silent before shaking my head and going into the kitchen. I opened the refrigerator door and as I bent down to grab a Corona from the shelf I heard the sound of Diamond's shoes tapping against the marble floor. I stood up, looked at her, and turned to open my beer. I brushed past her and walked toward the living room to sit down.

"So what are you planning on doing, Black?"

Damn, I didn't even get a second to plant my ass in a seat. She had already started. "I don't know yet, Diamond." I sighed as I spoke to let her know that I wasn't in the mood for this conversation.

"What do you mean, you don't know? You have to know. Are you just going to allow him to sneak up on you?"

"On me? Have you forgotten that you are the one that shot him? And you don't even know that it's him anyway."

"Who the hell else would it be, Black? It's the only thing that makes sense. When are you going to be a man and stand up to him?"

"What?" I was pissed. I got up from my seat, slammed the beer down onto the coffee table, and walked in her direction. I knew that she could see the anger on my face because she was backing into the corner of the sofa. "Be a man? Shit, I'm the man keeping your ass afloat. You wouldn't know what to do without me."

"Really? Well, you wouldn't have shit without me!"

Slap

Before I could think about it my hand had landed clean across the side of her face. She placed her hand over her cheek, which had quickly turned red. For the first time since we'd been together she'd pushed me to the limit. Now she sat across from me crying and I felt like shit.

"Babe, I'm sorry," I tried to reach out and grab her.

"Get the fuck off me!" She pulled her arm away and stood up from the sofa. I was going to try and apologize more but she gave me a stare that said if looks could kill I'd be dead. I never wanted her to see that side of me. In the past I'd snapped a few times and hit a woman, which is something that I wasn't proud of. I didn't even know what to say to fix it. *Shit*, I yelled. I sat there for the next half hour not even looking at TV. My mind was going in circles. I was pissed that I'd let this nigga ruin everything.

I remembered the first time that I saw her—I couldn't wait to get closer. I knew that I was going to be with her from that moment. I had come too far to fuck it up. I knew that I couldn't make it up to her tonight. I was so fucked-up about it that I called JB and told him to take care of the pickups that night. I didn't want to leave for fear that she wouldn't be there when I got back. At one point I crept upstairs and stood outside of the door listening to her cry. I was close to turning the knob and going in but it would probably have just made it worse. I had almost drifted off to sleep when the telephone rung. I jumped up, and glanced at the clock that read 4 A.M.

"Yo'," I spoke in a low tone. I knew whatever it was at this time of morning it couldn't be good.

"These niggas are trippin' out here, B, you need to come through and handle this shit," JB yelled into the receiver.

"What niggas?"

"Down on the block. Kenyon then went and put some shit in they ear and now niggas are tripping talking 'bout they can't trust you and shit."

I was pissed, I wasn't trying to hear that shit but deep down I knew it was coming. I could actually understand how they could feel the way they did. But shit, I was the boss running things so either they would get down or lay the fuck down, and that was my word. "I can't deal with this shit right now, JB. I got so much going on man. This shit with Kemp is fucking up my home life and everything. The way I feel now, I'll fuck around and blow his ass away. I need you to be a soldier and take care of it."

"I'm sorry to bother you but I didn't know how you wanted me to handle it. Is Diamond okay?"

"Naw man, I fucking snapped and I didn't mean to. She's been upstairs crying for hours."

"Damn, man, maybe you should go stay with Trice tonight."

"I'm not leaving, I just gotta get my head right. Shit is getting out of control."

"All right, well, call me when you get up in the A.M. I'm going to do another pick up now."

"All right," I replied before ending the call. I heard Diamond coming out of the bedroom and going into the bathroom. I felt like this was my cue. I walked up the steps and stood outside of the door. She opened it and was startled by my presence.

"Diamond"

She turned off the bathroom light and walked past me toward the bedroom. I followed behind her but didn't speak. She climbed into bed and pulled the blankets over her body. I had never seen her like this. I knew about the relationship she had with her ex Davey, and how he treated her. The way that he cheated and how they fought like cats and dogs. I could see by the way she looked at me how disappointed she was. I sat down in the chair opposite the bed and stared in her direction. As she closed her eyes and drifted off to sleep, I put my head back and closed my eyes too.

Chapter 5

Diamond

Spoiled Rotten

I opened my eyes and noticed Black asleep in the chair across from me. I was still angry about last night but regardless of his fuck-ups, I still had a soft spot for him. I knew he was sorry since any other night he'd be out running the streets. I sat up on the side of the bed and the sound of the box spring woke him up.

"Hey babe, you feel any better?" he said as he sat straight up. I was tempted to ignore him but I wanted to just get on with the day and let it go.

"I'm fine."

"Can I get you some breakfast or something?"

"No, I'm not hungry."

"You sure, 'cause I can get JB to drop something off or we can go to IHOP or something."

"I said I'm not hungry, Black—damn!" I got up from the bed and walked toward the door.

"I'm sorry, D, for everything."

I didn't say a word. I walked into the bathroom and closed the door. I had already decided that I would do some shopping today since shopping was the only thing that could help when I was upset. I did the morning ritual of brushing my teeth and washing my face. Black was gone when I came out. I let out a sigh of relief. I walked into the bedroom and saw a blue sheet of paper with writing on it. Next to it was a wad of money. I bent down to grab it. The note read, *I know I fucked up, but I'm going to make it up to you. I know shopping helps you clear your head when you're angry so here's a few dollars for you. Buy something nice on me.*

I smiled. He knew me well. Of course, I had my own money so I wasn't jumping for joy like I would have a few years back but I was smiling because he really wanted me to forgive him. I sat the note back down and grabbed my cell to text his phone. *I LOVE YOU* was all I wrote. I got dressed and headed out for my day of shopping. I opened the door and turned to close it and a tall, dark-skinned man was walking up the path. He was older, probably in his late forties. He had on a suit and dress shoes and was carrying a briefcase. I hoped my ass wasn't about to get subpoenaed to court or some shit.

"Hi, can I help you?" I asked, nervously.

"Yes, I'm trying to locate a Mrs. Diamond Brooks."

"Well, I'm Diamond, but my last name isn't Brooks any more. What can I do for you?"

"Don't I look familiar to you? Isn't there anything about me that looks familiar?" he said, as I stood there staring at him. I didn't really see anything that stuck out to me but there was obviously something he wanted me to see.

"No, really it doesn't. Is it supposed to?" I was still clueless.

"It's me Diamond, your dad."

My heart dropped at that moment. I mean, with all the shit

that I was going through at the moment someone would play a cruel-ass joke like this. I knew this couldn't be my father, I would have recognized him. Then he smiled, the smile that I couldn't forget, the same smile that I saw the day he disappeared from my life. *Was it really him?* What the hell was I supposed to do, hug him or slap him? I never thought that I'd see him again. I could have prepared what I would say but instead I stood in front of him, speechless.

"Are you okay?" he asked, breaking the silence.

I still stood, staring at him. I was trying to look deep inside of him, hoping I could get answers without asking. He'd been gone almost twelve years. Why would he come back now?

"I'm fine—actually no, I'm not. I'm trying to figure out why you're here." *Is that what I wanted to say?*

"I expected you to say that. You wouldn't be human if you didn't. I want to explain everything if you'll give me a chance to."

"How did you find out where I lived?"

"Through a private investigator," he replied.

"What? Why go through all the trouble? I mean, you left with no problem."

"I really want to explain and I don't think this is a good place. Could we go to lunch or something and talk?"

I wasn't truly ready to hear why he'd walked away. I had to figure out what to say to at least put the conversation off for another day. He stood there, waiting for my answer. The look on his face was so sincere, I could've almost been fooled, fooled into believing that he'd been there all the time or that he'd even been looking for me all of those years.

"I have an appointment in less than an hour, so could we meet tomorrow?"

He looked at me as if he were preparing to burst into tears. What was I missing? I mean, how could you miss me so much and stay gone so long? I wasn't trying to be mean at all but I wasn't going to be fooled into believing that I would have the void filled that had been empty for so long.

"There's no way you can fit me in today?"

I stood quiet for a few seconds before answering, I almost said yes. "Really, I can't. I have an important appointment that can't be missed."

"So is there a number I can call you at?"

"You've managed to find me this time, I'm sure it won't be hard to find me again." I turned and walked toward my car. I didn't want to turn around and see his face. Shit, I wanted him to feel the pain that I'd felt all of these years.

I got in the car, pulled my sunglasses down over my eyes, and drove away. Once I got around the corner I let go the tears that I had held in the entire time I stood in front of him. I had to tell someone but I wasn't sure how much of a shoulder Black could be for me to lean on at the time so I drove over to Kiki's office. Kiki, of course, had always been one of my best friends and was there in my times of need. Once I got all of the money from Kemp's death I bought Kiki her own bar. I wasn't about to have my best friend continue to work for tips at someone else's bar. The bar was a success from the grand opening and Kiki was where she needed to be, in charge. I pulled up in front of her office, which was located directly in back of the bar in Center City. I saw her car in front of the door so I knew that she was inside. She opened it before I even had a chance to get out and knock.

"I saw your car pull up, what's up, girl? I was going to call you today too."

I took off my sunglasses and displayed the drying tears on my cheeks. She walked over and hugged me.

"What the hell happened, is that nigga still acting up?"

"Girl, you won't believe who showed up on my doorstep today."

"Who?"

"My father," I said in a low tone. It almost brought tears to my eyes again.

"What? Girl, come on inside so we can sit down and talk. Your father though? Where the hell has he been?" she asked, while entering the door. I followed behind her and sat down in the first available chair.

"I don't know where the hell he's been. He says he found me through a private investigator. I didn't even know what to say, girl, I was standing there like a damn statue."

"I can't believe he had the audacity to just show up on your damn doorstep. He could have wrote a letter or some shit to see how you felt about seeing him. I mean, damn, people don't even think. He didn't even know if you wanted to see him."

"I was so shocked, like it's been over ten years. I'm not sure what he expected me to say."

"Shit, he probably didn't expect you to say anything. I mean, how could he? I think that's so inconsiderate what he did. Did you tell Black?"

"No, I haven't talked to Black and now that you mentioned it, he didn't respond to my text. I'm about to call him right now." I dialed his number, which went straight to voicemail. I was pissed. After the shit that had been going on lately I couldn't understand how he could turn off his fucking phone.

I screamed into the answering machine as soon as I heard the beep. "Just when I thought you were sorry you pull this shit! Why is your fucking phone off, Black? Call me when you get this damn message!"

Kiki sat at the desk, shaking her head. "What?" I asked with my face in knots.

"I don't know when you're gonna learn that niggas ain't never been shit and ain't never gonna be shit! You can't let that nigga get you all upset and shit, it's not worth it girl. I see I still have to be the mommy around here."

"Everything is just so messed up right now, Kiki, I gotta look over my shoulders and hope Kemp doesn't come blow my head off. I can't keep worrying about him all the time. I have to worry about me."

"That's the right idea!" She laughed.

I smiled but inside I felt like shit. I was lying. I was worried about him and of course even more worried about myself.

"Well, I'm headed to the mall so I'll get with you later," I said, before getting up and hugging her.

"Okay and remember what I said."

"I will, girl."

As soon as I got inside the car I pulled out my cell to call him again. As I entered the number the phone began to ring. It was Black.

"Yo', what's up?" His voice boomed even over the loud music that played in the background.

"Why the hell was your phone off?"

"It wasn't off, somebody else was calling at the same time. What's the problem?"

"The problem is that every time I need you here lately you're not available!"

"What the hell are you talking about, Diamond?"

"I need to talk to you about something—could you just come home?"

"I can't right now, you know that."

"Just like I thought, 'bye, Black!"

"Diamond?"

"What?" I responded angrily.

"I'll be there in a half."

"Okay," I smiled before hanging up. I knew what to say to get him home when I wanted him to be. He got home about five minutes short of the half hour that he'd promised. I was sitting on the sofa with the lights off. My mind was spinning and I didn't know how to stop it. I always thought that the day I finally saw my father, I'd hug him and the empty void that was there for so many years would be closed. Nothing ever turns out the way that I imagine, which always ended up being a huge disappointment. When I was disappointed, I always made stupid decisions.

Black walked in, looking around to find me. Once he noticed me sitting on the sofa he turned on the lamp and walked over.

"Babe, why are you sitting here in the dark? What's going on?" He sat down next to me.

"My father showed up today," I replied in a low tone.

"What?"

"Yes, I was leaving out and he was walking up the path."

"Well, what the hell did he say? I mean, why did he show up?"

"I don't know, he wanted to go to lunch but I lied and said I had somewhere important to be. I didn't know what to say. I couldn't stand to look at him after the way he left me."

"Well you shouldn't have been put in that position. I'm sorry you had to go through that shit today with all of the other shit going on." He moved closer to me and didn't say another word. I mean, there wasn't really anything that he could say. Him being there next to me was good enough. I lay in his arms on the sofa and closed my eyes. I could feel myself drifting off to sleep within seconds.

Chapter 6

Black

Eyes Behind My Head

Boom . . .

Debris was everywhere. All I could remember was sticking my hand on the handle to open up the car door and hearing a loud-ass boom and a force unlike any that I'd ever felt in my life. I landed up against the wall. My eyes were closed and I instantly felt the back of my head throbbing. I rubbed the back of my head, which felt like it was bleeding. What the fuck? I yelled. My car was sitting just a few feet away from me on fire. This shit was getting crazy! At this point I wanted this nigga to just show his face so we could get this shit over with. I heard sirens in the background as I tried to peel myself off of the pavement.

"Are you okay sir?" The one paramedic asked.

I couldn't even respond. I was still in shock and I was dizzy as hell with a banging headache. I tried to get up again.

"Stay still, sir, we'll get you to a hospital."

"I'm fine, I don't need a hospital."

"Sir, you have to go to a hospital, your head is bleeding and you could have a concussion."

"I said I'm fine." I tried to force myself up and fell right back down. I was pissed. "Damn!" I yelled in frustration. This nigga was really getting the best of me. My head was spinning and my legs were shaking. Before long, I was being put on the gurney, strapped down, and rolled into the back of the ambulance. The whole ride I kept asking to use the phone and they wouldn't allow me to. I needed to make sure that Diamond was okay.

"Please, can I call my girl? Whoever did this could be trying to hurt her."

The male paramedic didn't budge while the female paramedic immediately looked concerned.

"Do you have your phone?" she asked. Her male partner turned to look at her with a frown. She wasn't fazed.

"Yeah, it's in my left pocket."

She went in my pocket and retrieved the phone. "I can't unstrap you for safety reasons but I can dial it for you."

"Cool, her name's Diamond. It's in the phone book."

She dialed the number and placed the phone near my ear. "Hello?"

"Babe, are you okay?" I asked, breathing heavily. I had never been happier to hear her voice.

"Yeah, I'm fine, what's wrong with you?"

"Somebody put a bomb in my car but . . ."

"A bomb! Baby, are you hurt?"

"I'm okay, they're taking me to the hospital now. Don't run down here, I'm okay."

"I'm coming now."

"Babe . . ."

"What hospital are you going to? It's not up for discussion, Black."

"I think Penn," I replied. I knew there wasn't any arguing with her at this point.

"I'll meet you there." *Click!*

I looked over at the female paramedic and nodded my head in thanks. We arrived at the hospital where they hurried me into trauma. The whole time I repeated that I was fine and wanted to go home. My requests went unheard. After an hour of trying to fight them, they sedated me. The last thing I could remember was seeing a long-ass needle and heavy eyelids. When I woke up, Diamond was sitting in a chair at the bedside.

"Hey, Babe, how are you feeling?" She got up from the chair and came over to sit next to me.

"I'm good."

"What the hell happened?"

"Somebody put a bomb in the car and . . ."

"A bomb?"

"Listen, don't get bent all out of shape. I'm okay as you can see."

"You could have been killed. We have to get away from here, babe."

"I'm not running from that nigga, fuck him! If he's coming, I'm waiting."

"You see what keeps happening? He's going to kill one of us." I could tell how afraid she was. What the hell was I supposed to say? There probably wasn't anything that I could say to ease her mind. I thought about what she said and it made perfect sense, getting away. I wasn't about to run but I needed to get her out of harm's way. Even if just for a week or two, it would give me time to sort things out.

"Look, I'm going to send you away for a couple of weeks. See if Kiki can get free and go with you," I said as I sat up in bed. I knew sending her away without me wouldn't be easy. I prepared myself for an argument.

"What? Why the hell would I go away and leave you here? If I go anywhere you're going with me."

"I'm not going to argue with you, D. I'm angry, my fucking car is blown to shreds, and my head hurts like hell. If you stay here you're a target and I need time to figure this shit out. I need you to listen to me for once and stop being so damn stubborn."

She sat there with a blank stare. I was waiting for her to yell, cry or do something other than sit in silence. I could see how this was affecting her. Diamond had always been strong, since I'd known her, anyway. That was one of the things that attracted me to her. I knew that she wouldn't let a nigga run over her. Now, things were different. She was falling apart and I didn't know how else to patch her back together other that killing this nigga. Soon a single tear formed in the well of her right eye, slowly rolled down her cheek, and dropped onto the sheets.

"I'm losing my mind, Black, I can't take this shit. I thought I was built for this. It's much easier when you're the predator. I can't believe that I was so stupid."

"Don't beat yourself up about the past, okay. I need you to think realistically, babe. You shot that nigga and he could have lived. Shit, if that were me, I'd be doing the same shit. I know him well and if it's him I know he won't stop until he gets what he wants. I would lose my mind if I lost you."

After a few seconds of silence she spoke again. "Okay, I'll go."

"I'm glad." I smiled as I reached over to hug her. I wasn't trying to get sentimental but on some real shit, I needed her in my life. She was the balance that I never had before. I know that it may sound fucked up since she was once and still may be my best friend's wife, but he didn't deserve her. Hell, he didn't give a fuck about her. I remember the first time they'd had sex up in the box at the Sixers game. No sooner than he closed the door behind her he was boasting. I had never been one to brag about getting ass, but Kemp, he needed to feel like a king. That day she had finally gotten his attention. She'd been trying for weeks and he knew it.

"I need to make her sweat. Shit, that gold-digging bitch ain't about to get a piece of me that easily." He laughed. "She's sexy as shit but I know the game."

"How you know she playing you? She could really like you."

"Bullshit, Black," he began to laugh. "That bitch just got out of jail, she's broke as hell and who the fuck goes around practically stalking a nigga if it ain't about money. You sound like one of them. You ain't getting soft on me now, are you?"

"Soft, come on man, I'm far from that. I'm just saying, you gotta stop treating every female you meet like a gold digger just because you rich."

He continued to laugh, "What you trying to say, it's real love out here?"

"That's exactly what I'm saying."

"Nigga, I've been married twice and I'm divorced. These bitches only see the dollars. If I was a chick I'd be the same way."

"You're divorced because you think like you do. You only got married 'cause you're selfish."

"And I already know that shit, man. I lock 'em down, that's how you gotta do it. And Diamond, she'll be number three. If you know one thing about me it's that I keep my promises, and I promise you that shit."

He couldn't wait to clown her after he fucked her with all of us sitting a few short feet away. She left out of the room with a huge smile on her face. As soon as the door was closed, everyone but me burst into laughter.

"You ain't right, man," I spoke loudly. Everyone turned to look at me as if I was speaking in another language. To them, I was. There were just some things that I couldn't accept as right—shit, I had three sisters.

"Yo', you been acting like a bitch lately. You act like you want to fuck her. You know me, nigga, I don't cock block. If that's what you want by all means go for it," Kemp yelled. Everyone turned to look at me and soon erupted into laughter.

"Come on now, don't try to play me, nigga. You know it ain't that. I'm just saying, why you gotta come out here and boast. Everybody knows you get pussy!" I was getting annoyed. If it was one thing I hated, it was to be put on blast, especially in front of a bunch of niggas.

"Stop tripping, man, if it makes you feel any better I'll refrain from talking about pussy around you." He continued to laugh.

I didn't even respond. I just nodded my head and took a sip of my Corona. Soon the attention was off of me and back on the game. I sat there wondering how this dude even got to where he was at that point. I mean, he was street smart and he had the wit to get all of the shit he had, but keeping it—that was a whole different story. That took more than what

he had and I could see him losing it even back then. I didn't
envy Kemp but I did always want to claim his spot. Even as his
friend, there was something in the back of my mind. I could
see the future and was ready to jump in his place as soon as
it was open.

Chapter 7

Diamond

Permanent Monday

Who the hell was at the door so damn early? I thought while crawling out of bed. Black was asleep next to me and hadn't budged even after the bell rang a fourth time. I put on a robe and headed downstairs. I looked out of the peephole and spoke.

"Who is it?"

"Hey, Diamond, it's your dad. Can I come in and talk to you for a minute?"

"Right now isn't a real good time, you should have called first."

"You didn't give me your number."

Damn, I wasn't ready to talk with him yet but I knew that he'd keep trying until I did. "Okay, let me put something on, give me a minute," I replied, hoping that by the time I got back down to the door he'd be gone. Once I got up to the room, Black was sitting up on the side of the bed.

"Who's at the door?"

"My father."

"Did you let him in?"

"No, not yet, I came up to get something on. He's still standing outside."

"You should have just let him in."

"I am going to let him in, damn!" I yelled. He looked at me and shook his head.

"I'm sorry okay? I know it's a sore subject."

"I'm sorry for snapping. I'm going to go see what he has to say to get this over with. He's not going to leave me alone until I do."

"Well, I'm going to jump into the shower and head out. If you need me, holla!"

"Where are you going? You're not supposed to be in the streets. The doctor said to rest for a week. It's only been three days, Black."

"Go ahead and talk to your dad. I'm fine, okay."

I didn't respond, I just grabbed my shorts and slipped them on before leaving back out of the room and down the stairs again. I glanced out of the peephole again to find him patiently waiting on my return. I took a deep breath and opened it.

"Thanks a lot for talking to me, Diamond. There are some things I just have to explain."

I took a few steps back to give him room to enter. As soon as he did he looked around with a pleased look. I guess he was proud of what I had accomplished—well, at least I hoped that he was. I always wanted his approval after he'd gone away. I blamed myself for his departure. I thought that I wasn't good enough. I prayed for him to come back so I could prove that I was. Maybe this was my chance and the longer I thought about having the satisfaction of being loved by him the happier I got.

"This is very nice, Diamond, you're doing well. I'm happy about that," he said as he walked into the living room and sat down.

"Thanks," I replied, joining him on the sofa. "So what is it that you wanted to talk to me about?" I went straight in. I'd waited for this day for so long and now that I was ready to know the answer I couldn't wait any longer.

"Well, it's about us and why I left."

"Us? What do you mean by that?"

"About me being your father."

I sat there still unsure of what it was he was trying to say. "Okay and what about that?" I asked with a confused expression on my face. I was hoping that he hadn't come to bullshit me. I wanted him to get to the point and stop beating around the bush.

"That I'm your biological father."

"What? Mom told me that I was adopted." Okay, so now I was getting annoyed. I wondered if this was just a ploy to get close to my money.

"You were adopted, by her."

"I still don't get what you're trying to tell me. Excuse me if I'm a little slow this morning, but I need you to get to the point."

"After your mom and I were married, I had an affair. It lasted about two years and I didn't tell your mother about the infidelity until my mistress became pregnant. It hurt her and I had never felt worse in my life. Well, Nila couldn't have children and she'd always talked about adopting. Pam, the woman I had an affair with, didn't want children but I convinced her to go through with it promising that I'd leave Nila.

Once you were born she tried to be a mother, but it wasn't in her. She couldn't take care of you, especially without me. I couldn't and I wouldn't leave Nila at that time so we all decided that we'd let her adopt you and Pam would move on with her life." He stopped for a few seconds. By then, tears were flowing. If this was all true that made the fact that he'd walked away from me even worse. I was his biological daughter?

"I don't know what to say. I mean, that still doesn't explain why you walked out on me."

"Because I was in love with Pam and Nila promised me if I walked out on her I'd never see you again."

"So I'm assuming that means you chose her over me, right?" Now I was angry. I couldn't believe what I was hearing. Nothing was making sense.

"I didn't choose her over you, I love you and I've always loved you from the day you were born and I held you in my arms. I wasn't happy and I couldn't be the father you needed if I stayed."

"I still can't believe what I'm hearing. It really took you ten years to tell me this?"

Just as he was about to speak Black came down the stairs. My father stood up to greet him.

"Black, this is my father Jim, this is Black, my . . ."

"Fiancé, I'm Black her fiancé," he interrupted me, while reaching out to shake his hand.

My fiancé? Was I missing something? When the hell did that happen?

"Nice to meet you, Black, is that your real name?"

He had nerve, like he wanted to act like a father now. What the fuck did he know about being a father?

"Naw, my real name is Keshawn Black but everyone calls me Black."

"Oh, okay."

"Well, it was nice meeting you, Jim. Babe, I'm gonna run, call me if you need anything." He leaned in to kiss me. I didn't know what he was thinking but I'd definitely discuss it with him later.

"Okay," I replied. I didn't want to let on that I was upset. I was trying to be strong.

Black left and I immediately turned my attention back to my father. He had sat back down on the sofa but remained quiet.

"So what do you expect from me? I still don't understand the purpose of this meeting." I wasn't slow but I just didn't know how he could walk in here after all this time, tell me a story like he'd just done, and think I'd run and jump in his arms like I used to as a child.

"I wanted you to know the truth. You haven't asked about Pam—do you want to know what happened to her?"

"Why? She didn't want me. Why should I give a damn about her?" My face was twisted so tight my head was beginning to hurt. What kind of woman would do that? Here I believed that my mother was weak for falling apart like she did. Hell, who wouldn't under those circumstances?

"That's not true, she loves you."

"How do you know that?"

"Because I've been married to her for the past eight years, and she's only stayed away because she thought you wouldn't want to see her."

"That's bullshit! You know I can't believe that you all lied to me. My whole fucking life's been a lie." I stood up from the chair and paced the room. "So what's next, huh? I guess you're going to tell me you had kids, right? I mean that's next right?"

He was quiet. I shook my head and masked my tears with anger.

"I'm sorry, Diamond, I really wish I could turn back the hands of time and fix this."

"Get out!" I yelled.

"Diamond, please"

I turned my back and hoped that he wouldn't speak another word. Soon I heard his footsteps and the door closing behind him. I burst into tears as soon as the door shut. Just when I thought things couldn't get any worse he dropped that bomb on me. I didn't know what to do or who to call. My mind was racing. My biological mother—the one I never thought of seeing before—and my asshole of a father had left me out to dry. Where the hell was he when my mom was strung out on drugs? Where the hell was he when I fell into depression after Johnny went to prison? Where the hell was he every time I needed him? I was hurting and confused. I sat down on the sofa and placed my face in the palms of my hands. The phone rang a few minutes later and startled me. It was Black.

"Babe, how'd everything go?"

"Crazy, my mind is racing over here. I told him to get out. I can't believe the shit that he just told me."

"Do you need me to come home?"

I wanted him to be there, but honestly, I needed time alone to clear my head. I didn't want to end up taking my anger out on him. I was quiet for a second before speaking for fear that I'd say the wrong thing, which I often did when I was upset.

"Honestly, I just need to be alone right now. I appreciate you asking. I want to talk to you about it but right now I'm still trying to take it all in. I'll see you tonight when you come in and we'll talk then. Is that okay?"

"Whatever you want, babe. If you change your mind, call me. I'll call and check on you in a little while."

"Okay, I love you."

"I love you too."

I'd never felt a pain as deep as the one I was feeling at that moment. I knew he wouldn't listen and would probably be on his way back home to see what the hell was going on. Being alone was what I thought I needed but most likely wasn't the case. I thought about my mother and how special she was. I mean, a woman who could take care of a child that her husband went outside of their marriage and created was extraordinary. I loved her before but even more at this moment. I tried to fit in and it never really mattered. I continued to cry until Black walked through the door and held me. Breaking down was a sign of weakness and lately I felt myself slipping. I felt like something was taking over me and I hated it. I struggled to tell Black all that I'd just heard from my father. He comforted me until I was calm enough to begin drifting off to sleep.

Chapter 8

Black

New Money

"Yo', what's taking this nigga so long? He called over an hour ago. How long does it take to drive from G-town?" I was getting annoyed. I was waiting on Kenyon to bring me the money from last night's pickup. I should have stopped fucking with him the day I saw how he felt about Kemp but I let it slide because he was a good worker. JB and I were sitting inside the warehouse for way too long. I'd called his phone six times and hadn't gotten a response yet.

"You want me to call him again?" JB asked, noticing my frustration.

"I already called that muthafucker six times, he's gonna make me bust a cap in his ass for real!"

JB sat there quiet, glancing down at his phone. You could cut the tension in the room with a knife. I felt like I was losing control of them since they believed Kemp was alive. I had to figure out a way to get my soldiers back in line even if it meant permanently getting rid of the bad seeds. One thing that stood out about this situation was a comment Kemp once made to me. It was back in 2002 and things on the strip had never been better. We were killing all the other local crews in sales and were slowly taking over. Of course with more money comes more jealousy and envy. I always knew it but had never witnessed it myself. I thought that if there were any form of hate it would come from the outside. Everyone that worked for Kemp was paid pretty well—maybe not as much as he was or as much as they wished they should have been—but it was well in my books. They never wanted for anything, or at least that's what I thought.

Back then there was a runner named Tony that handled most of the money pickups. He'd known Kemp since they were kids and had actually been one of his best friends. Money began to come up short and it didn't take long to figure out where the money was going. Kemp confronted Tony when he came to the warehouse to drop off the money.

"How much is this?" Kemp asked. You could tell Tony was nervous but he tried to maintain his cool. Kemp remained calm.

"Ten thousand."

"Ten? You sure?"

"Yeah, I counted it myself before I came here."

"I called and got report and it should be thirteen so you sure about that?" Kemp got up from his chair. I was sitting in a chair off to the side, unsure of what was about to go down. Kemp wasn't one to discuss what he planned to do. Most times I don't think he even had a plan. He seemed to do things at the spur of the moment.

"I'm sure—who the hell said it was thirteen? I counted ten."

"It doesn't matter who said it, what matters is the three Gs that's missing."

"This is bullshit, Kemp, you know me better than that. Why would I steal from you?"

"I've been trying to figure that shit out and I'm stuck. I make sure you get dough and this is the thanks I get?"

"I keep trying to tell you I didn't steal from you. If anything's missing you need to holla at them niggas on the street." Tony was now raising his voice. If there was one thing about Kemp that never changed it was that once his mind was made up it was pretty close to impossible to change it.

"Well, I don't believe you," he shouted while reaching to the small of his back and retrieving his gun. "I trusted you, nigga, and I guess that was me being naïve. I'm not about to let you get away with that shit. No one steals from me." He was now pointing the gun in his direction. I was still sitting in the chair waiting for what would happen next. I mean, I was pretty sure what was about to happen but I wasn't sure what Kemp would do afterward.

"If you gonna shoot me then get it over with, you'll feel like an ass once you find out it wasn't me!" Tony yelled back. You could tell Kemp didn't really want to shoot him by the look in his eyes. He looked at him like a brother.

"Me feel like an ass? That'll never happen. You should feel like an ass for thinking that you could get away with this bullshit!" he yelled. His finger was now firmly on the trigger. His face was in knots and his eyes showed the anger that was flowing through his body. A few seconds later, he shot him twice in the chest. His body fell into the wall behind him and slid down to the floor. Blood was smeared down the wall and forming a puddle beneath Tony's body on the floor.

"Damn, this shit gonna fuck up my carpet!" Kemp said before putting his gun down on the desk. I still hadn't budged. I was waiting for him to give me an order. He walked over to the phone and dialed. I didn't know who he was calling at the time but I'd find out a few minutes later. "Help me wrap this nigga up, they're coming to get him in a few minutes."

I got up from the chair and helped him wrap Tony's body up in plastic. I was still in shock. I had seen Kemp kill before but never someone as close to him as Tony. He was trying to prove a point, which was that it didn't matter who it was—if he was crossed—they would be taken care of. To me, this was a valuable lesson, which would aid me in situations like these. Kemp taught me that you couldn't trust anyone regardless of how close you were to them.

As I stood here waiting for Kenyon, all I could think about was Kemp and this lesson. Though Kenyon wasn't close to me, he was one of the workers and I didn't trust him as far as I could throw him. He didn't respect me the way that he did Kemp and I felt like I had to prove a point. I wanted people to fear me the same way they feared him. My mind was racing as I dialed his number one last time. He still didn't answer. A minute or two later I heard footsteps nearing the door.

"Yo', what the fuck took you so long?" I yelled as soon as his face was revealed through the opened door.

"My bad, I got caught up with some personal shit. I'm here now, here's the money," he said walking over to the desk and dropping the black duffel bag full of money on the table.

"Personal? What personal shit would you be handling while you're carrying my money?"

"I said my bad, damn! All the money is there." He pointed to the bag.

I walked over to him and stood close enough where he could most likely feel the heat from my body. "Don't let that shit happen again."

"All right, it won't." He stood firm in his position as if he didn't fear me. This added fuel to the fire but I relaxed. I didn't want him to know he was pissing me off. "Do you need me for anything else?"

"I'm not done talking—why the fuck are you cutting me off?"

"I'm not cutting you off, I just have some shit to handle. If you don't need anything else I can go take care of it."

"I didn't say I was finished, I'm still trying to figure out why you would make a detour with my money."

"I've already said *my bad*, I'm not gonna keep saying it, man. It won't happen again." Kenyon was getting angry which only pissed me off more. Why the fuck was he angry? To me that meant he had something to hide.

"Who are you yelling at? You don't have any reason to be upset, you're the one lollygagging with my fuckin' money in the wings. You should have dropped that shit off first." I was repeating myself and I hated it. I just wanted to make sure this nigga knew not to play games with me.

"Look, I'm not no sucka Black, you're not gonna be talking to me like some fucking young boy. I told you what happened and that's that. You don't have to keep repeating yourself either because I heard."

I felt just like Kemp did when he faced Tony that day. I wanted to blow him away but I had to think about it. Was killing him going to prove anything? I couldn't let him disrespect me like that, though I would definitely lose more respect like that. I'd worked too hard to gain what I had and I'd be damned if I'd let one nigga ruin it. "I'll talk to you however I see fit. You work for me, nigga, don't ever forget that!" I yelled.

"How can I? You keep reminding me."

His sarcasm was taking me to a level of anger that I was trying to avoid. My fingers were gripped tightly around the .45 that was in my hand. Sweat was forming on my forehead from the adrenaline rushing through my body. JB was sitting there with his eyes glued to Kenyon's back. He was waiting for one of us to make a move. I couldn't even respond to what he'd just said. He didn't respect me and it didn't matter what I did at this point. For me, there was only one option: killing him. With a quick hand motion, I raised the gun and shot him in the chest. He stumbled before I released four more shots, forcing him down to the ground. JB didn't budget, almost as if he knew what I was about to do before I did it. I gave him a look, which meant get help to come take him out. I walked back to the desk and sat down. I placed the gun on the desk and grabbed a cloth to wipe the blood that I felt resting on my face.

JB left out of the office and shortly returned with a couple of the runners, some rope, and a bunch of plastic. I still sat silent at the desk. I hated the fact that I had to resort to murder. I hoped that I could keep him around regardless of his attitude toward me after he believed Kemp was alive. He actually was a good soldier his loyalty just didn't lie with me. After they wrapped him up and took him out of the room the female we used to clean up messes like these came in and begin cleaning up the blood that was left behind. I got up to leave the room and walked straight into JB, who was on his way back in.

"I know this ain't a good time, but it's somebody I want you to meet."

"You're right, it ain't a good time, so can we do this later?"

"I wish we could, but with Kenyon being gone I need you to meet this dude like yesterday."

"I just shot this nigga and you're already trying to replace him."

"Well, what am I supposed to do? I can't handle the work on both ends alone."

I stood there for a second thinking. He was right, I couldn't expect him to handle Kenyon's area. He had to be replaced or shit would get out of hand. At this point I had to think rationally if I wanted things to get back on track. Putting too much work on one person would only hurt the situation. "All right, where is he?"

"Out front, his name is Money."

"Money? I think I heard that name before. Is he the one that holds down the corner outside of Papi's?"

"Yeah, that's him," JB said as we walked toward the exit. I couldn't remember where I knew him from at the time but I knew that it would come back to me eventually. We exited the building where Money was standing, leaning up against a Ranger Rover. I was impressed; for a nigga that holds down one corner he seemed to be doing especially well. It also made me wonder what the hell he needed me for. Naturally, I was a suspicious dude but I figured I'd give him the benefit of the doubt since I trusted JB.

"Money, this is Black. Black, meet Money."

I reached my right hand out to shake his. I nodded my head before speaking. "So JB tells me that you want to work for me."

"Well, I was thinking more like a partnership. I do pretty well on my own block so I definitely don't want to work for anyone. I figured we could work together to knock all the other hustlers out of the box."

What the fuck is he talking about? I thought. Why the hell would I begin a partnership with a nigga I don't even know? I must look like a straight fool.

"A partnership? What makes you think I need a partner?"

"I didn't say you needed one, but you could only benefit from having me on your team. I know you don't know me and if a nigga I ain't know came to me the same way I'd be skeptical too. But on some real shit, I'm one of the toughest soldiers out here. You won't find another me, for sure."

"Maybe we can work something out. I'm not sure if it'll be a partnership but I'll figure it out once I get my head straight. I got a lot of shit on my mind right now and I can't really make that kind of decision. Give JB your contact information and I will get back to you by the end of the week." Though most of what I said was true. I wanted to wait until I did a little research. I didn't really trust what he was saying. I didn't want to hear too much more of his pitch because him being my partner was out of the question. Niggas like JB had been down with me from day one and I hadn't given them that opportunity. They'd look at me like an asshole if I let this nigga slide in so easily.

"Cool, I appreciate it," he said, reaching out to shake my hand.

"I'm out, JB, call me if something's up. I'll be back shortly."
I walked over to my car and began my drive home. I had so
much on my mind and so much to straighten out. I had just
killed someone. In the past I'd shot at a couple of people and
had hit a few but had never killed anyone. It was a different
feeling, one of triumph. I felt like I could do anything at that
point and I planned on using this no-tolerance method from
that point on.

Chapter 9

Diamond

Where I Belong

I sat on the steps, both eyes full of tears. They had just handcuffed Johnny and took him off to jail. I was losing my best friend and there wasn't anything that I could do to stop it. Did I cause this? If I hadn't pushed him so hard maybe this wouldn't have happened. I could remember the blood all over him and he ran to my house to tell me what happened. It was a vision that I'd never be able to erase. I heard banging on the back door. It was almost midnight so I knew it could only be him. By the sound of the knocks I could tell that something was wrong so I hurried to the door to answer it. It was pouring outside and he stood there in jeans and a T-shirt soaked with rain and blood. He stood there frozen as I stood on the other side of the threshold with the same look.

"What the hell happened, Johnny?" I said as tears instantly formed in the wells of my eyes. I grabbed hold of him to make sure that he wasn't hurt.

"I did it, I couldn't take it anymore. I did it," he said as he walked through the door and began pacing. Water was dripping all over the place, leaving little blood-tinged puddles all over the kitchen floor. He was disoriented and filled with anger. I had never seen him so upset. Each time I tried to touch him he'd snatch away and keep repeating the same thing over and over again. I didn't know what it was that he'd done at that moment but I knew it couldn't be good.

"Babe, what did you do?" I was crying at this point. I wanted to console him but at the young age of sixteen I didn't know how. I thought about movies and TV shows to see if I could remember how they'd done it. My mind was drawing a blank and my instinct wasn't helping much either.

"I did it, I fuckin' killed him. I did it."

"Who did you kill?"

"My father, he can't hurt us anymore."

I couldn't believe what I was hearing. Did he just say he killed his father? The only thing I could think of doing was holding him. I wrapped my arms around him and held on tight as we cried together. I felt like my world was crashing down. He was going to be taken away and I'd probably never see him again.

"It's all my fault, I'm so sorry."

"It's not your fault. I had to. I couldn't let him keep abusing us. I had to stand up and be a man."

Stand up and be a man was what I'd always told him. I told him that he'd never be a man if he couldn't stand up for himself and protect his sister. I pushed him and now his life was over. I stood there holding him close without saying a word until I heard police sirens and saw flashing lights. A few seconds later there was banging at the door. I opened the door after Johnny gave me a nod. The cops pushed me aside and burst into the house, immediately putting handcuffs on him. My mother and aunt had since woke up and were standing in the living room with me. My mom was clueless as they dragged him out of the house. I cried and tried to free myself from my mom's grip to get one last hug. He was out of the house and into the car before I could get to him. I sat on the steps looking on as they drove away. My head was buried in my knees.

"Come on in, baby, and get out of those pajamas, you're soaked."

I didn't budge as if I was glued to the steps. My body felt like I was drained of the energy that I had. "Diamond, come on, sweetie it's late and you have school tomorrow."

School? Was she serious? I'd just witnessed something that would probably stay with me forever. The look in his eyes when he spoke those words reminded me of those serial killers in movies. There was no feeling behind it. It was as if he didn't care that the man he'd just killed was his father. How could you murder someone and not give a damn? I know that he did it to save them from abuse but even still, he should have cared. After a while my mother just sat down beside me and placed her hand on my back. I sat there until I was all cried out and exhausted so much so that I had to lie down.

I didn't get up for school the following morning or the rest of that week. I cried all day and night. I wanted to close my eyes and wake up and it would all be gone. I wanted to be able to hold him at night when he'd sneak over and make love to me. I wanted to laugh with him and smile when he told me how much he loved me. I missed my best friend and letters would never fill the void.

Now all of these years later I realized how much I needed

a father. I didn't know it back then but I knew now how important it was to have him around at times like those. My mother tried but I was never as close to her as I was to him. I missed him being there to console me when I was upset so when he walked away I felt the same way I did the night they took Johnny away.

I thought about it long and hard. I had to talk to my real mother and figure out why she gave me away. The explanation that my father gave me wasn't quite enough for me. I mean, I had come to the realization years ago that my mother didn't want me but with the information my father had given me I felt a lot different. I always prayed that I would meet her and finally feel like I was somewhere that I belonged, but once I heard the words that were coming out of my father's mouth I didn't quite feel the same. I was hurt. It was a hurt that I couldn't really explain. I couldn't imagine a pain much worse than this. To know that I was the result of an affair and then to be dumped by the woman that ruined a happy home was worse than just being rejected. Even if she had just given me up for adoption and disappeared I wouldn't have felt as bad as I did. She not only left me fatherless but motherless. The only mother that I'd known pretty much committed suicide because she was so stressed about their breakup. I believe that any woman would be devastated about taking care of her husband's love child to keep their marriage together only for him to leave anyway.

I told my father that I wanted to meet both him and Pam together. There were a lot of unanswered questions and some things that I needed to say. I wanted them to know how they ruined my life. I wasn't going to let them back into my life that easy. They needed to suffer the way that I had all of the years that they were gone. Black tried to talk me out of it, saying that I didn't want to dig too deep because I'd most likely find out things that I didn't want to know. I didn't care honestly, I needed to know where I came from. Even if it hurt, I'd figure out a way to get over it just like every obstacle that had been thrown my way.

I told them that I would come over to their house for dinner. I was nervous especially since I would be meeting Pam for the first time. What would she look like? How would she react to seeing me? There were so many questions going through my mind I could hardly relax on the drive over.

I arrived at a large row home in the Northeast part of Philly. There were two cars in the driveway, a black Lexus and a white Acura. *Somebody must be doing pretty well,* I thought. I wasn't going to jump to conclusions but if they were over here living well while we struggled in North Philly all of those years I'd be disgusted. I parked on the side street and walked over to the door. I almost turned back around but the motion lights came on. I didn't want to get caught running away from the door so I stayed. I rang the bell and heard footsteps nearing on the opposite side.

"Glad you made it," my father said, opening the door with a huge-ass Kool-Aid smile on his face. "Come on in," he motioned with his hand.

I slowly walked inside and took a quick survey of the area. Everything was perfect, not even a pillow was out of place. I moved in just enough for him to close the door and stood still.

"Don't be scared to go in further. We won't bite." He laughed.

I didn't join in. This wasn't a situation that I could laugh about. I didn't find anything humorous about meeting up with them.

"Pam, she's here!" he yelled out. A few moments later I heard shoes clicking against the hardwood floor. When I saw her face I knew—I knew that I belonged to her. She was beautiful and had a body that was pretty close to flawless. She had a bright smile with perfect white teeth and long, silky hair. I was almost her spitting image. I stared at her from head to toe. She was dressed in designer gear and flaunted diamonds everywhere. She looked exactly as I hoped I would when I reached her age.

Tears streaming down her face soon joined her smile. She walked over to me and wrapped her arms around me. I was hesitant about hugging her back. Eventually I gave in but it wasn't genuine, not on my part anyway. I felt like hugging her back was the right thing to do at the time.

"I never thought I'd get a chance to see you this way. I wanted this day for so long."

She backed away while holding onto one of my hands and looking me up and down. "You're so pretty, you look just like me when I was your age."

I still stood there, silent. I wanted to thank her for the compliment but something in me wouldn't allow me to.

"Come on in the living room so we can sit down and talk," she said slightly pulling me in the direction of the living room. I followed behind her and took a seat on the sofa opposite of the love seat where she sat. I still wasn't all that comfortable.

"Before you start to speak, I just need to say a few things." I had finally broken my silence. I wanted to just get it over with. "I want you to know that I'm angry first and hurt second. I'm angry because it took this long for you to reach out to me. I needed you both when I was a teenager getting into trouble because my mom was too busy getting strung out to pay me any attention. Or when my aunt would get angry and starve me all day while parading food in front of my face. Or when I fell for a worthless man and ended up spending nine months in jail. There were so many times in my life that I needed you and you were nowhere around. Looking around here, you seem to be pretty well-off, so it disgusts me that you would leave me in that tore-down neighborhood all of those years. Did you even know that I went to jail? I went to jail for nine months because I desperately wanted a man. I felt like there was something missing from my life. I needed a father and a mother. Yeah, my mother was there but she was high on drugs. You caused that and you should feel bad because now she's dead. The only mother that I ever knew is gone. I'm not sure what it is that we'd want to gain from this meeting. An apology would fall on deaf ears because it can't erase all of the crap that I went through." I paused for a second to catch my breath. I was finally getting the chance to speak my mind.

"I know that you said an apology wouldn't matter, but I am really sorry. I was young and dumb back then. I got caught up in an affair and wasn't ready for a child. I honestly did what I thought was best for you. If I could turn back the hands of time I would, but being with me might not have been the best thing for either of us."

I sat quietly and listened to what she had to say. Maybe there was some truth to what she said. I mean, who knows what would have happened if she would have kept me. Though I couldn't think of being in a more fucked-up situation than I was in, you never really know. I was trying to keep an open mind even though I was angry.

"Diamond, I never wanted to leave you but Nila didn't give me a choice."

"You can't sit here and blame it all on her. There's no way a judge would have left me with a drug addict and not placed me with my biological parents. So I'm not a fool, you can't try to convince me of that."

"I know you're not a fool. I believe that you're a very smart woman. But you have to believe me. I really wanted to take you away but one side wanted to keep you and the other side didn't."

"So I'm assuming the side that didn't want to keep me was her, right?" I spoke aloud.

"It's not that I didn't want you, I couldn't take care of you." Pam jumped in and spoke in her defense. "I really wanted to be with you and it killed me to watch you grow up from afar and not be a part of that. Though I wasn't around, I kept up with you. I always knew what was going on in your life."

I was starting to believe her. Either she was a good actress or what she was saying was truly genuine. "So how many other children do you have?"

"We only have one other child, his name is Javan."

"How old is he?" I was finally breaking the ice and slowly getting over the anger and wanted to know more about the life that I missed. Although I was kind of jealous I instantly felt close to him and felt an urge to meet him.

"He's nineteen, he goes to college at Temple."

"Wow, so I have a brother. That's crazy." I was still taking the idea in. I always wished I had a sibling. I wanted that just as much as wanted my father. "So when can I meet him?" I could tell by their reaction that they weren't expecting me to say that.

"You really want to see him?" Pam asked.

"Yes I do." I wasn't sure where I wanted to take this relationship with them but I did feel that it was important for my brother and me to get acquainted.

"So what does that mean for us?" my father asked. I figured that would be his next question.

"I honestly don't know. I wish that I could give you an answer but this is a situation where we'll just have to take things one day at a time."

"That's fair and I respect that. We just want a chance and if you decide to pull away we'll accept it," my father said grabbing hold of my hand. I almost pulled away but decided to allow the affection. After all, it's what I longed for.

"So how about you give me your number to give to Javan so he can call you. I'm so excited for him. He's always wanted to meet you," Pam said with a huge smile across her face.

"So he knew about me?"

"Of course, I never wanted to hide you. All of my family knows about you."

I felt myself warming up even more. I had a whole family out there that I didn't know anything about. I couldn't wait to meet them. "Well, I have to get going. I told Black that I'd meet up with him." I stood up and began to move toward the door.

"You're leaving so soon? I thought that you would have at least stayed for dinner."

"No, I have some things to do but I will come back. Now that I'm around we have a lot of catching up to do." I laughed. I was really interested in learning more about them so I planned to stay around.

"Well, drive safely," my father spoke quietly as if he was sad that I had to leave. I was actually sad I was leaving as well. I wanted to stay and find out more about them but I couldn't.

I gave them both a hug and headed out of the door, down the driveway, and into my car. They stood at the door, waving good-bye as if I was going off to college or something. The entire time I sat there talking to them I felt my anger slipping away. All my life I was bitter and angry with the people who gave me away. The fact that I didn't know the whole story didn't help. I wondered why my mother kept them away from me all of those years or why she never fully revealed the situations surrounding my adoption. I'd never know the answer to that and at this point it didn't really matter. I was where I belonged and where I should have been all along.

Chapter 10

Black

Motives

"So where you from?" I was sitting at my desk opposite of Money. I still didn't trust him so I was trying to feel him out. I had started my research and I wanted to test him to see if I'd catch him in a lie. Word on the street was how much of a hustler he was. He was known to work hard to maintain. Never flashy, which was a good quality. He had a Range and a few jewels but he didn't over-do it like most niggas with money do when they get on. To me, that meant that people wouldn't be so fast to test him and if I was going to have him on my team I needed to know that I could trust him with my goods and money. He sat across from me with a stone-cold face. I figured he was trying to show me that he wasn't afraid of me.

"From Frankford, I hold down the block up there."

"You hold down a block where you live?" I replied. That was definitely the wrong move.

"Naw, I said that's where I'm from not where I live. I don't tell nobody where I live, not even you."

I was taken aback by that response. What the fuck did he mean, not even me? If I wanted to know I could find out.

"How long you been hustling? You look pretty young."

"Shit, I've been on the block for three years. I'm not trying to make a career out of hugging the block, though. I just want to get enough ends so I can get out of town."

"So three years and you still on the same block alone. You should have people out working for you by now."

"I don't trust a lot of people and I'm not trying to pay niggas to do some shit that I can do better by myself."

"I can respect that," I said, nodding my head. "So what is it that you think you can enhance by being part of my team? If you've done so well working alone for all of these years, why partner up with someone now? Unless you have an ulterior motive or something, it just doesn't make sense to me."

He smiled. "Nothing like that. I have some connections that no one in Philly has. The product that I sell is like fifty percent cheaper than the lowest price you'll get."

"fifty percent? I'd have to see that to believe it."

"I wouldn't bullshit you. That's why I manage to make so much money out here alone."

"I'm still confused. If the profit is so great why share it with me? You don't know me from Adam." I sat there with a dead stare. I was anxious to see what he'd come up with next. He'd answered most of my questions in a clever fashion, almost as if he'd rehearsed it. I couldn't quite put my finger on what was bugging me about this dude. Something was sticking out like a sore thumb and I had to figure it out.

"Yeah, I don't know you personally, but I've been watching you for awhile. I like your style. I mean, I think the way you took over after Kemp got murdered was remarkable."

What the hell? Did this nigga just say he's been watching

me? I wasn't too comfortable with that. Then he makes a comment about Kemp. Where did that come from? "Watching me?"

"Yeah, not like no stalker," He burst into laughter. "From a distance and from the words of the street. I feel like I've known you for years and we just met. You remind me of myself and I like that."

I laughed a little myself. There wasn't anything else I could do but laugh. He was cracking me up and the fact that he was dead serious made it that much more comical. He didn't appear to appreciate my humor. "I like you, Money. And I'm cracking-up because I've never met one nigga that would have the balls to come at me the way you did. That shows me that you have heart."

He nodded his head as his frown loosened up a little bit. "Cool—so do we have a deal or what?"

"You gotta tell me the perks first. All you said was about a connection. You still haven't said what you'd gain from hooking me up with your connect."

"I mean, you have a huge customer base and that's what I'm trying to get. If we work together, shit, we can take over the whole city. You feel me?"

He was really starting to make sense now. I was down for a takeover. In fact, that had always been one of my goals. I had the power that I wanted now. I just had to figure out the best way to use it. "Cool, give me a few days to sleep on it and I will get back to you."

"Okay, well, thanks for meeting with me. I appreciate you hearing me out." He got up to shake my hand. I got up from my chair and obliged.

"I'll be in touch."

He nodded and turned to leave the office. JB rushed in no sooner than he made it out of the door. He closed the door behind him and came rushing to my desk.

"Yo', what the hell are you so hype for?" I asked. He was looking like a crackhead fiendin' for some crack.

"I'm just anxious to see how the meeting went."

"Why, are you getting a cut or something?"

"Come on man, I'm just looking out for you."

"For me?" I burst into laughter. Who the hell did he think he was fooling? "It's all love, man. The meeting went okay, I told him to give me a couple of days to sleep on it." I could tell JB wasn't too happy about my answer and I couldn't fig- ure out why. Maybe I was being a little insecure or maybe my nerves were getting the best of me. I trusted JB as much as I possibly could in this situation.

"Okay, just don't let this good opportunity slip away."

"I'm no fool JB, I got this."

"All right then. I have to go make a couple of drops so I will get up with you later."

"All right." I reached out to shake his hand.

After he walked out of the office I sat there thinking about Money's proposition. I was definitely leaning toward going with his idea but I couldn't let him know so fast and seem des- perate. With me, everything was planned. Shit, I even planned what underwear I'd put on. Every move had to be calculated because one slip could end it all. The phone rang just as I was getting up to leave the office. It was Trice. I hadn't seen or communicated with her in a couple weeks and I knew she'd be pissed.

"Hello," I said in a low tone.

"Where the hell have you been? I'm glad that you're alive, which lets me know you were just avoiding me for the past few weeks."

"I wasn't avoiding you, I just had some personal shit to deal with."

"Like what, Diamond?"

"Come on with that, Trice, I'm not gonna argue with you right now."

"I'm not going to either. You keep pushing me away and Diamond's going to end up getting her feelings hurt."

"What? Don't fuck with me, Trice, besides Diamond ain't the type of woman that'll let shit like that affect her. I don't even know why you're going there. You act like you are my girl or something."

"So what am I, then? What have I been for all of these years?"

"I'm not even going to answer that question, Trice. On some real shit, this conversation is giving me a headache."

"Don't come running to me when she leaves your ass!"

Click!

She hung up and I was glad. Threatening me damn sure wasn't about to make me run into her arms. I don't know why she believed that she was anything more to me than pussy and the mother of my child. I used her to ease my mind and to get a release when my mind was out of sorts. I couldn't focus on her at the moment; she'd be back. This was just one of her stunts. Every time she felt like I was neglecting her, this happened. I mean, don't get me wrong, Trice was the shit in bed and could potentially make a great woman but I had

Diamond. See, Trice I met back when I first began hustling with Kemp. I was parked outside of the corner store laughing and talking shit with a few of the guys. She walked by with her friend Cherrie and everyone including Kemp was trying to holla. I stood in the back and gave her a few smiles and she threw a few back at me. She had a dark tone, smooth skin, and her body was the shit. Her curves fit her long, lean legs, and her breast sat up like gravity hadn't taken its toll. I waited until she stepped away, allowing Kemp to talk to her girlfriend. I walked over and moved close to her. I wanted her to feel the heat from my body and smell the aroma of my Gaultier cologne. I could tell she was getting sucked in the minute I was staring her eye to eye.

"I saw you giving me the look so I figured I'd move closer so you wouldn't have to strain your eyes looking at me."

She giggled. "Up close and personal is the way I like it." She was flirting and I liked it.

"So what's your name?"

"Shartrice, but Trice is fine."

"Well, Trice, it's nice to meet you. My name is Black."

"I know," she said, smiling.

"How do you know that?" I asked, surprised. I know I was a well-known nigga but not like that.

"Everybody knows Black—you and Kemp are the talk of the town."

"Oh, really? Well, I guess that's a good thing." I hunched my shoulders. "So when are you gonna let me take you out to dinner or something?"

"Whenever you want."

"Well, what if I said tonight?"

"Then I'd say, see you later." She smiled and tapped me on the chest with her finger. She was turning me on. There was no way I could resist.

"Cool, give me your number and I'll call you around eight to come scoop you up."

She wrote her number down on a small sheet of paper and slowly placed it in the palm of my hand. She turned to walk away, giving me a perfect view of her ass. I called her that night but instead of going out to dinner, I ate her, if you know what I mean. It was on and poppin' after that with Trice. We were actually a couple at one point and I was ecstatic when she had my son. Shit just went down the tubes after that. We argued a lot, mainly because she wanted me to marry her and I wasn't into that shit back then. So she goes out and cheats and gets pregnant by another nigga. What type of shit is that? She actually thought shit between us would be the same after that. I was still angry about that shit but I did have genuine feelings for her that even my anger couldn't erase. Before I got with Diamond, I contemplated being with her but she couldn't handle my lifestyle. Diamond was used to it and she was the type of woman that could handle anything that was thrown her way. Trice would fall apart at the mere glimpse of drama. I had to have a strong woman on my team and though I felt bad for leaving her to raise my son, I did my part so that he'd never want for anything.

So I didn't believe Trice would do anything to mess up her life. But there's always a possibility, which was proven when Diamond called my phone an hour after I got off the phone with Trice.

"Why the fuck is your baby moms playing with me? I told

you before to get that bitch in check because I will gladly go over there and whoop her ass!" she yelled into the phone.

"What did she do now?"

"This bitch called me talking about how you're still fucking her and you're planning on leaving me to be with her."

"That's bullshit, Diamond, I don't know why you even feed into her dumb shit. She's just mad because I didn't fuck her. I'll straighten her out later."

"No, you need to straighten her out now before she gets hurt. If it wasn't for your son I'd shoot that bitch! She's not going to keep disrespecting me."

"Calm down, Diamond, it's not that serious."

"It's not serious to you but it is to me! She's not calling you with the dumb shit she's calling me."

"How do you know she's not calling me?"

"Oh, so you've been talking to her?" she said with attitude. I could almost imagine the expression that she had on her face.

"Yeah, I talk to her, she is the mother of my child. Let's not do this, Diamond, please. My head is still hurting from arguing with her."

"Are you being smart?"

"No, Diamond, my head is hurting. I'm on my way home to lay down for a little bit."

"All right I'll see you when you get here."

Click!

Chapter 11

Diamond

Love Lockdown

Since that last incident with Trice a couple of weeks ago things with Black and me had been better. I decided that I wasn't about to let him slip away or waste my time fighting with some chick that he didn't even want. In all actuality she wasn't any competition. There wasn't a chick around as fly as me. Yeah, she had his baby but I had his heart and I wasn't letting it go no matter how hard I had to fight to keep it. I realized how much his son meant to him and I wasn't trying to stand in the way of that but I had to get him where I wanted him. When it came to planning, I was the queen. Shit, she could try but I had a defense for every attack in the book. So I sat around thinking of a way that I could grab him hook, line, and sinker. I came up with the answer: having his child. I had never thought of having a child before now but I knew how much that meant to him. I wanted to keep the kind of control that Trice had. Shit, even if we weren't together he'd still be around. Unlike Trice, I didn't need him for money, I needed him for power. What we had took both of us to maintain. When Kemp died I was left with properties and numerous businesses, including an auto-body shop, a few corner stores, a barbershop and hair salon. Though I had more than enough money to keep up living the lavish life we were used to, Black needed to be in control. It's sort of like a boy waiting his whole life to run the family business. Black waited in the wings for the chance to walk in Kemp's shoes and now that the door was wide open there was no way I could pull him away from it. Honestly, I wasn't sure that I wanted to. There were some things about the business that I didn't like—the women, the late nights, and the threats. But just as I hated those things I loved the fact that it made him happy to finally be in charge. He was in his element, no longer having someone telling him what to do and how high to jump. I could never understand how he worked for Kemp as long as he had but I guess his loyalty meant more.

Finally knowing my family was also something that pushed me toward having children because family was more important to me now than ever. Now that I had a family I didn't want to let go.

I was on birth control for as long as I could remember. When I ended up knocked up as a teen my mom put me on pills. In a way, I was glad because I loved my life too much to have to deal with a child back then. I stopped taking my pills consistently right after the last argument we had about Trice. I'd flush one down the toilet every other day so he wouldn't find out that I wasn't taking them. I knew that it would take some time for them to work but I knew when I was most fertile and I made sure that we got it in during that time.

Two months went by and I was still getting my period. I was pissed. I felt like the longer this dragged on the possibility of it happening was slimmer. I decided to let Kiki in on my plan. It was hard for me to keep her in the dark. I pretty much told her everything even when I knew she'd try to talk me out of whatever crazy idea it was I had at the time. I drove over to her house unexpectedly and noticed JB's car parked in the driveway. *What the fuck?* Since when is Kiki cool with JB? I started to leave since she appeared to have company but after a few seconds of contemplating I ended up going to the door anyway. I knocked lightly and waited patiently. A few seconds later Kiki's voice screamed from the opposite side of the door.

"Who is it?"

"It's D, girl, open the door."

"Give me a second, okay."

Now I knew she was in there messing around. I laughed to myself as I stood outside of the door. Miss I-don't-date-drug-dealers was caught in the act. I wanted to see her lie herself out of this one. After five minutes I knocked again but this time not so lightly. Unexpectedly the door opened and JB was standing there putting his jacket on.

"What's up, Diamond?"

"I should be asking you that question." I laughed. He smiled and walked past me. Kiki was now standing at the door with a devilish grin on her face.

"Don't even say anything, girl, just get in here."

"I'm cracking-up inside, let me just tell you that. You are funny as hell." I smiled as I walked inside and headed over to the couch. "So what's the deal? You and JB—I would have never imagined that."

"Yeah, me either, girl, you know how I feel about them drug-dealing niggas. I don't want to have to sleep with one eye open waiting for someone to do a drive-by and shit. I'm lo-key. Damn shame he can lay the pipe, girl."

I burst into laughter. "JB, really? He don't look like the type."

"Well, his looks are definitely deceiving."

"How the hell did you even hook up with him? I never even saw y'all talking before."

"He was down at the club a few weeks ago and kicked a little game. I almost ignored his ass until he gave me a hundred-dollar tip. I figured I could at least go out with him. Going out turned into fucking and we've been doing it ever since." She laughed and slapped me a high five.

I was all for Kiki finding a man; she'd been single for a while now. It was good to see someone making her smile for a change.

"So enough about me, what brings you here? I know it wasn't to say hi—you never come all the way over here for that."

She knew me so well. "Well, I came over to tell you about my plan. I know you're going to try and talk me out of it but I can't keep secrets from you."

"You always got a damn plan girl. Your mind's always wandering. What the hell are you up to now? I hope it ain't anything illegal, you can't afford to go to jail again."

"No, not illegal, but conniving as hell."

She sat back in the chair and gave me a funny look. Her eyebrows were raised and her smile was a little smaller than it had been a few minutes earlier. "I stopped my birth control pills."

"What? Why the hell would you do that? You are in the

prime of your life. You damn sure don't need to be dragging no baby around. Plus that shit drops your sexy ratings by at least two points."

"Sexy ratings? What the hell are you talking about, Kiki?"

"The way niggas look at you, duh!"

"Girl, I'm focused. I'm gonna have Black's baby and bump that bitch Trice out of the picture."

She laughed, "What? I know you can come up with a better plan than that. Shit ain't like that baby will guarantee he'll stay. The only thing that will guarantee is that you'll be tied up with a whining-ass kid every day. Girl, I can't even think about that."

"I didn't know you were so anti-child."

"I love kids—don't get me wrong—but just somebody else's."

"Well, that's my plan and I'm sticking to it. All I have to do is get knocked up."

"That should be the easy part. You really think that chick is going to give up that easily? I don't see it. She's stuck around even after he dumped her ass for you."

"It ain't about what I think; it's about what I know. And I know that bitch won't have a choice."

"Okay now we don't need no more murders."

"I'm not trying to go there, Kiki, but you know I will."

"I didn't know you cared about Black that much, honestly. I thought that shit was just another game."

"I love him and I know he loves me. Girl he called me his fiancée when I introduced him to my dad."

"Your dad? When the hell was that? I see you've been keeping me out of the loop lately." She sat up in the chair.

"I've just been busy. You know you're my girl, I can't keep shit from you."

"Okay then spill it."

"Well, I went over and met my mother and I look so much like her. I mean, I could almost be her twin. It turned out a lot better than I thought it would at first. I almost didn't go because I was scared of what I would see. I was actually surprised. I warmed up to them pretty fast. It felt like I belonged, you know." I was getting choked up just talking about it.

"Wow, I'm so happy for you D. I know that means so much to you."

"It does. I have a brother too, named Javan. I haven't met him yet but I did talk to him on the phone."

"That's so good."

"Yeah, but back to my plan."

"You never cease to amaze me." she laughed.

"I'm serious about this, I'm really ready to do this."

"I hope it works for you. I don't want to see you get hurt and to bring a baby into this world to be caught in the middle of all of that drama isn't good. But I got your back whatever you decide to do. You know that." She moved over to hug me. I felt better knowing that she had my back. I didn't doubt it but I still needed to have it confirmed. "So where are you off to?"

"Home to my man, girl, gotta get working on this baby!" I yelled. We both giggled as we walked to the door. I gave her one more hug before leaving. I dialed Black's cell and didn't get an answer so I left a message. I drove home hoping he'd call before I got there. I turned the corner and saw his car parked outside. I smiled. I parked, got out, and went inside. I went upstairs after calling his name a few times and found him asleep across the bed with the remote control in his hand.

"Babe," I said as I tapped him on the leg. He woke up, startled.

"What's up? Damn, I was knocked out."

"Yeah, snoring and all."

"No, I wasn't, stop lying," he said, smiling. I always picked with him about snoring. I told him I'd tape him one day so he could hear it for himself. He looked at me almost as if he could eat me. Hell, I wanted him to eat me, to be honest. I wanted to jump on him and make this baby that I wanted.

"Come here," he said reaching his arms out to grab me. His warm hands wrapped around my waist. His fingertips were caressing the small of my back and his lips were kissing my cleavage. I moaned a little, confirming how good he made me feel. I pushed him back onto the bed playfully. He smiled. He loved it when I took control. I didn't say a word, only loosening his belt and unbuttoning his pants. His dick was already hard and practically busting through his jeans. Once I pulled his pants and boxers off and revealed his dick, my mouth began to water. I was extremely horny, so much so that my pussy juices were soaking up my panties. I grabbed hold of it and gently planted a kiss on the head of it. I kissed it a few more times before taking it in my mouth. As I sucked up and down I used one hand to jerk it and the other hand to massage his balls. I'd occasionally take it out of my mouth and spit on it. He said shit like that turned him on. He was begging me to stop but I couldn't—well, I wouldn't stop. I was too focused on getting every drop of his cum in me. After a few more minutes I stood up, removed my pants and panties, and climbed on top of him. His dick went inside of me with ease. I was so wet each time I'd slam my ass down a splashing effect occurred.

"This pussy is so wet," he moaned.

I didn't respond, I kept riding him, moving my hips in circles and fitting all of his length inside of me. I would occasionally stop for a second just to bend down and kiss him. He'd kiss me and as I'd go to sit back up he'd grab hold of me to kiss a little more. As we lay stomach to stomach I'd slowly lift my ass up and push it back down. I'd grind and moan at the same time. Though the moans were muffled by our passionate kiss you could still hear them escaping into the air. Over the next half hour and a continuous pace he erupted inside of me. Both of our bodies were shaking and exhausted. After I crawled off of him we lay there quiet. I was on my back staring up at the ceiling with my mind wandering. I hoped that this session of love making would get me the results that I yearned for. Black was quiet as well and I knew if he were ever quiet it meant that he was in deep thought. Most times I'd let him be rather than interrupting him but this time I wanted to know what was on his mind.

"Why are you so quiet? What's on your mind?" I said as I turned on my side and rubbed my hand across his chest.

"Just thinking about this dude named Money JB recommended to me."

"Money? That name sounds familiar."

"Familiar how?" He turned to look at me.

"I don't know, it just sounds like I heard it before."

"Well, he's trying to partner up with me and I'm leaning toward doing just that."

"Partner? Why would you need a partner?"

"I don't need a partner technically but he has some connections that will only benefit us in the long run."

"What's wrong with the connections that we already have? I mean, with this Kemp shit still lingering do you really trust dealing with somebody new?"

"I'm not worried about Kemp and this doesn't have anything to do with him and whoever is out here trying to scare us the shit ain't working. I'm not about to stop my money because of that shit. This can only put more money in both of our pockets. I know that you love money so what's the problem?"

"There isn't a problem. I just want you to be safe. I'd die if something happened to you."

"Nothing's going to happen to me." He turned on his side and was now staring me in the eyes. This was one of those sensitive moments that I treasured. He placed his hand on the side of my face and rubbed it gently. "I love you, okay. I'm not about to go down that easily."

I smiled and kissed him. I knew that he loved me and I had him where I wanted him. The pregnancy would seal the deal. With that, I'd permanently have his love locked down.

Chapter 12

Black

More Drama

"Why the hell do I have to argue with you all the time? It's not like you want for anything!" I yelled. Trice was standing on the opposite side of the room with her hands on her hips and her face frowned up.

"Who said I didn't want for anything? I want us. I want things to be the way they used to be. I don't know what's so special about her. I tried to hang around hoping that you'd see her true colors and dump her ass but I can't do this anymore."

"What colors? You don't even know her."

"Not personally but I know all about her. How could you be with someone like her?"

"I'm not going to explain that, Trice. The bottom line is I'm with her and that's that."

She sat there with a sad look on her face. I never wanted to hurt her but what the hell was I supposed to do. Don't get me wrong I did love Trice but not enough to go back. That's partly what made me look at her as if she were just a piece of ass when I needed some. I could admit that her actions were

partly my fault since I never told her how deep my relationship with Diamond really was. I was going to marry her and it
was probably about time I told her.

"I can't accept that."

"Well, you'll have to because soon I'm going to marry her."

She stared at me as if she was ready to cry. I'd just broken
her heart in a million pieces. How did things get this way? I
still couldn't figure it out. As men, we make some of the dumb-
est choices when it comes to dealing with women. Not saying
that being with Diamond wasn't the right choice, just saying
that leading Trice on was. Unexpectedly she grabbed a vase
off the table and threw it at me. It just missed my head by
inches and crashed against the wall behind me, breaking into
pieces. Tears were pouring out of her eyes.

"Get the fuck out!" she screamed.

"Trice, I'm . . ."

"Just get out, please. I can't stand to look at you right now."

I turned to walk toward the door without a fight. She'd
come back around eventually, she always did. I opened the
door and said, "I'm sorry" before walking out. Once I got inside the car I reached in the glove compartment and pulled
out the little black box that I'd just picked up from jewelers
row. Inside was the five-karat engagement ring that I bought
for Diamond. I didn't think that the time was right to pro-
pose to her because if Kemp was in fact still alive, she couldn't
marry me anyway. I took the ring out the box, glanced at it for
a few seconds, and put it back inside. What was I going to do?
My mind was going in circles as I looked up at Trice standing
in the window. We made eye contact for a few seconds before
I turned on the car and backed out of the driveway.

Kemp was now on my mind more than ever. Almost three months had passed since the car bomb. Not that I wanted something else to happen but I was ready for war. I was tired of waiting around like a sitting duck for him to sneak up on me. I was ready to go to war and get the shit over with. I pulled my cell phone from my jacket pocket and dialed Tommy. I hadn't seen him much in the past few weeks. Kenyon was his right hand, so with him missing I knew he'd probably blame me.

"Hello!" he yelled over the loud music in the background.

"Yo' it's Black, what's the deal?"

He turned down the radio. "Nothing, man, what's up?"

"I should be asking you that question, where you been? I ain't seen you in a minute. You got that much dough you ain't gotta work no more?"

"Naw man, I was just feeling under the weather. Had to take some time to get myself together that's all. I'm gonna get back on my job this week."

"Is that right?"

"Yeah, I wouldn't bullshit you."

"For as long as I've known you, you've been about money, so this disappearing act seems pretty strange to me. This wouldn't have anything to do with Kemp would it?"

"Kemp? Hell no, I don't believe everything I hear in the streets. I really don't believe he's alive. If he were alive he would have showed his face by now."

He was right; Kemp wasn't afraid of no one. I couldn't see him doing all this shit and hiding in the background. Kemp was more on point too—shit, if he wanted me dead I would have been dead by now. My mind was seriously playing tricks on me.

"All right man, just get with me this week."

"I will, yo', have you heard from Kenyon? I've been calling him and I ain't get no answer."

"No, I haven't. I was just about to call him too," I lied.

"Last time I spoke to him he was on his way to see you."

"Damn, well, I ain't never see him. Did you stop by his crib?"

"Yup, his car ain't even there."

"Well, I'll ask around too, if you hear anything let me know," I said, acting as if I was concerned. I knew exactly where he was, in the damn river where he belonged. That nigga should have been more loyal and the way Tommy was acting he'd probably end up right there with his ass.

"Cool," he replied before ending the call.

I had one more stop to make before going home. I looked in my rearview mirror and noticed a black Lincoln behind me. It was almost eight o'clock so it was dark outside. I could see that there was just one person in the car, the driver. I felt like I was being followed because each time I switched lanes or made a turn they did the same thing. When I'd speed up they would be right on my bumper. I was getting angry. I got on the highway to head to South Philly rather than taking the streets. It was Saturday so the roads wouldn't be so empty. If someone was in fact following me I didn't think they'd be bold enough to do something in front of all of those cars.

I got on and merged into traffic. The black car followed right behind me. I knew for a fact they were following me at that point. I drove at a steady speed until I reached my exit and as I was going off I was hit in the back. I almost lost control but I got it together quickly. Glancing in my mirror I now saw two people when there had only been one the last time I looked back. I sped off, even going through red lights and all. I was nearing one of my stores when the passenger leaned out of the window and began firing shots. One pierced the back window then a few more hit the body.

"Fuck," I yelled. I grabbed my cell phone off the seat while trying to speed through traffic. I dialed JB. I was close by the block that he ran so I knew he'd be around. He picked up on the second ring.

"Hello."

"These niggas is shooting at me I'm coming around the block now." I dropped the phone. I knocked my driver-side mirror off. I was making it through small streets while they were still following behind me. Where the fuck were the cops when you needed them? As I neared the block I looked behind me and noticed the car was gone. I didn't even notice that they had turned off. My heart was racing. Just when I thought this shit was dying down it comes right back. JB and a few niggas were standing on the corner when I pulled up. You could smell burning rubber from the tires. I jumped out of the car as they all ran over to examine it.

"What the fuck happened? Who was following you?"

"Hell if I know. When I first noticed the car it was one nigga. I get hit in the back, lose control for a second and look back it's two niggas in there." I was pacing and yelling. I was so mad. I could've been shot that time. It could've been all over for me. I wasn't even about to tell Diamond what happened so she could get all upset.

"Damn man, you gotta start riding with someone until this shit gets straight. Did you see what kind of car it was?" JB asked, now angry himself.

"It was a black Caddy. I'm so fucking mad right now. I'm going to need to use someone's car. I can't drive this shit home like that. D will have a fit."

"Take mine. I'll get that shit fixed for you in the A.M."

"All right, I'll get up with you in a few hours. I have to take care of something real quick."

"All right," he responded before shaking my hand.

I jumped in his car and quickly sped off. I was pissed. What the hell were they going to do next? How many times would I be able to escape death? I'd been lucky so far but maybe JB was right, I needed to have someone riding with me at all times. I felt like a sucker needing a bodyguard but I wasn't ready to die. I wasn't going down that easily. I couldn't even think straight; I completely forgot about the stop but fuck it I'd just get to it later. I had to go regroup. I was paranoid, looking in the rearview mirror every few seconds. I pulled up in front of the house and sat there for a minute or two to get myself together. I didn't want Diamond to know something was wrong. I had always been pretty good at hiding things from women but lately it hadn't been working out that way. Before I could get out the car and up to the door she was standing there with the door wide open, tapping her feet on the ground.

"What's wrong with you? Why are you sitting out here like that?"

"Nothing is wrong, I was coming in."

"You never sit out here like that unless something is wrong. What's going on, Black?"

"I said nothing, D, chill out."

"I'm not going to chill out until you tell me what's going on. Did Kemp try to get at you again?"

"What? What the hell would make you say that?" I tried to fake it, hoping that sooner or later she'd give up or believe me. At least that was what I was hoping for.

"First of all, you're in JB's car and you were sitting out here with your head down like something heavy was weighing on your mind. I'm not a fool, Black."

"I got a flat so JB let me hold his car until the morning, okay? Stop reading so much into everything. I said that there wasn't anything wrong." By this time I had brushed past her and made it into the house. She was still standing there with the door open. "Could you get in here and close the door, please?"

She closed the door but still kept a frown on her face. I walked over to the sofa and sat down. I wasn't going to give in and tell her what had gone down. I'd have to hear her mouth all night if I did.

"I'm not slow, Black, I know you too well," she said before coming over to the sofa and sitting beside me. I was sitting there with my head back and my eyes closed. I loved Diamond but I hated the fact that she could never leave well enough alone.

"Diamond, please, I have a headache and you're not making it any better."

"Well, let me go get you some aspirin," she said getting up.

"Thank you," I replied.

She returned to the room a few seconds later. I soon felt cold water and a bottle of aspirin hitting my face.

"I'm not an asshole, and just 'cause you get in some fight with your little bitch out there you don't have to act all funny with me."

"What the hell is wrong with you, Diamond?" I yelled, sitting up and wiping the water off of my face. Where the hell did she get that? "This doesn't have anything to do with anyone, Diamond, my fucking head is hurting and I thought I could lay my head down for a little while. Obviously I was wrong when a nigga can't rest in his own fucking house," I yelled. "And thanks for the aspirin," I said before throwing them back at her and heading toward the steps. I turned back to look at her before I walked upstairs. She was standing there still angry. I sighed and shook my head as I took the steps. I felt bad for snapping but not bad enough to apologize. She had to stop being so damn persistent before she got an answer that she didn't want to hear. I went up to the bedroom, shut the door, and lay down. I was trying to clear all of the drama out of my mind at least for an hour or two. Surprisingly, Diamond allowed me to rest without bothering me. When I woke up to head back out to the house she was asleep on the living room sofa. I left her untouched and snuck out the door. It was time to get back to work and it was also time to finish this war that had begun. I wasn't going to hide and I damn sure wasn't going to run. I'd get at him and whoever was down for him. Just like Kenyon, Kemp and his help were going down.

Chapter 13

Diamond

Emotional

My moods were so up and down. One minute I was laughing and shedding tears the next. It was like something out of a horror film. I felt like one of those psychiatric patients that you see on TV. I was sitting in the tub relaxing. Black was out working as usual and lately we'd argued more than usual. I wasn't sure if it was the stress or if it was someone else. I mean, I knew he fucked around but it seemed like this situation was weighing him down. I had to do something to get his mind back on me, which is where it belonged. Then I thought about it, I hadn't gotten my period yet. I hurried and washed up and got dressed quickly so I could drive to the CVS and grab a pregnancy test. With all of the arguing I had completely forgotten that I was trying to get pregnant. Plus, I'd been unsuccessful for so long that I thought it wouldn't work anyway. I had a big smile on my face as I went to the counter to pay for it. The chick at the register gave me a funny look. Instead of snapping like I normally would I kill her with kindness.

I couldn't get home fast enough I was so excited. I dropped my purse downstairs and hurried up to the bathroom. I paced for the few minutes it took to show the answer that I was hoping for: pregnant. Though I had been waiting for this moment for the last few months I never knew how I'd feel once I found out. I hadn't prepared that part of the plan. How could you really prepare yourself mentally for something like this? Within five minutes I'd went from anxious to happy to nervous. *What the hell was going on with me?* I thought. I had to pull myself together. I was always a fighter. I always stuck to my plans no matter how crazy they might have seemed.

I had to let it sink in for a few more days before telling Black. I decided to run by Kiki's to let her in on the news. As I was leaving out of the house, my cell phone rang. It almost startled me. It was a number that I didn't recognize. I almost didn't answer it but I said what the hell and picked up.

"Hello."

"Can I speak with Diamond?"

"Speaking, who's this?"

"This is Trice," she said loudly. *How the hell did she get my number?* I thought. I damn sure wasn't in the mood to be fighting with this chick.

"How can I help you?"

"Look, I know that we haven't gotten along in the past but I wanted to know if we could meet somewhere and sit down and talk."

"Talk? About what? Any other time you're jumping down my throat or screaming obscenities."

"And I'm trying to move past that."

I didn't trust her one bit but with all of the other shit going on in my life I could stand to lose one enemy. I wondered if this reconciliation was an act or was it truly genuine.

"Well, I'm pretty busy this week but maybe one day next week."

"Are you sure that you can't squeeze it in this week?"

What the fuck was the rush? I felt like she was up to something. I didn't know Trice too well but she seemed desperate and I wasn't in the mood for any tricks.

"No, I can't," I replied sternly. Shit, if she wanted to meet it would be on my time.

"All right then, I'll give you a call back next week. Oh, and could we keep this between us? Black will swear I'm up to something." She gave a girlish giggle.

Was she serious? Don't tell Black? She was definitely up to something now. She'd just confirmed it for sure. "Okay, no problem," I lied. I was damn sure going to tell him. I wasn't a fool. I hung up and shook my head. I couldn't even wrap my mind around what had just happened. Now she's trying to be all friendly. A week ago we would have been in a full-blown argument before I got a chance to say hello. Thinking back, her hatred never had anything to do with me. I definitely believed that Black was dipping and dabbing though he'd swear to God he wasn't. I mean, unless you were a total nutcase you wouldn't bring so much drama for nothing.

When Black and me first got together I made sure that everything was on the table. If there was one thing I hated, it was surprises. He told me that he didn't have a woman but his son's mom was one of those die-hard women that wouldn't let go. Of course I was cocky and I felt that even if he was going back and forth what I had would keep him with me. Besides, when they were together she went and had a baby by another dude. I thought for sure he'd never want her. The more she called and tried to cause drama between us the more I saw how much she cared about him. It didn't matter how many times he'd cuss her out or throw me in her face, she'd keep coming back for more.

I left out of the house and got in the car. On my way over Kiki's I was blasting my new Beyoncé CD. I was singing alone like I was in a full concert. I stopped at a light on Broad Street and for a second I thought I was seeing things. I saw a female that looked just like Mica. I swear she could have been her twin. The car sped by me; it was a blue Camry. I was still trying to look back at the car when the car in back of me began to beep because the light had turned green. I was losing my mind. I laughed out loud as I pulled off. I made it to Kiki's in record time and of course I damn near knocked the door down banging. I was always impatient when I had something to tell her.

"I knew it had to be you. No one else has the balls to knock on my door so damn hard." She laughed.

"I have something to tell you—well, actually I have a few things to tell you. Girl, you know I saw some chick that looked just like Mica when I was on my way over here?" I was babbling on as I made my way into her apartment and closed the door behind me. She'd walked into her living room before me and sat down on the sofa.

"Mica? Girl, I know you're tripping. That girl is cremated and poured out in the ocean. I know that ain't what you came all the way over here to tell me," she said, lighting up a cigarette.

"Girl, you need to stop smoking. You saw that damn commercial with all the people falling out in the street and shit.

That's gonna be your ass if you don't quit. You're gonna be just like that man playing the guitar with the electronic voice." I burst into laughter. I was laughing so hard tears came to my eyes.

"That's not funny," she replied.

"Well, how about Black's baby mom called my damn cell phone talking about she wants to meet up so we can talk. I don't know what the hell she has up her sleeve but she don't know me. She's gonna fuck around and get herself hurt. Shit, I'm the queen at this conniving shit—she betta ask somebody," I said, slapping Kiki a high five.

"I can't believe that she called you. She's up to something, you better tell Black to get her ass in check."

"I know right. I'm so sick of that girl I don't know what to do."

"I mean, when is she going to get the point?"

"Oh, she gets the point now, that's why she's trying to be my friend."

Kiki and I both laughed. "So when the hell is he going to get you a ring? Shit, he's already claiming you as his fiancée."

"Well, that leads to what else I came to tell you. It worked girl, I'm pregnant!" I yelled. She sat there for a second before responding.

"Wow, I can't believe it. You really did it, you are nuts, girl!" She put her cigarette into the ashtray and blew out some smoke before reaching her arms out. "Well, looks like I'm going to be an auntie. I'm so excited!" She yelled as she hugged me.

"I thought I'd be jumping for joy when I found out but it was weird. I couldn't get my emotions together. I'm actually afraid to tell Black."

"Why, he'll be happy. He loves you, girl."

"I know but I'm not sure if now is the right time. Maybe I was being selfish, you know. I felt him slipping away. I can't lose him to her."

"Her who? His BM? Girl, if he wanted to be with her he would be."

"I know—well, at least I hope," I said as I put my head down.

"Girl, don't sit around here and get sad after that good news. That's the best thing I've heard all day." She laughed and slapped me on the leg. She was right, it wasn't a reason to be moping around.

"I just have to figure out how I'm going to tell him."

"Shit, just tell him. Catch him off guard with it."

"Oh, it's going to be off guard. Shit, I never even mentioned wanting kids before."

"So are you sure you really want this baby or is it primarily to keep him?"

I sat quiet. Really, I didn't know the answer to that question. In a way I wanted to do nothing more than have a baby with the man that I love but I did want to keep Black. So was I wrong for deciding to do things this way? I was the type that would do whatever I have to do to get what it was that I wanted.

"I would say that it was a combination of the two."

"Well, you know that I'm always here for advice and hopefully it leans more toward the side that you're doing it because you want to."

"It is," I lied. That wasn't really the case but I felt like saying that it was would end the conversation. I wanted her to be happy for me just as much as I wanted to be happy myself.

Was I really happy? I don't know, but that was something that I would have to explore. I couldn't change my mind now since it was already done. I wasn't going to get an abortion after all of the trouble that I went through to get pregnant in the first place. That would most likely bring back some old memories that I'd worked hard to suppress anyway. I stayed and chatted with Kiki for about another half hour before I hugged her good-bye and left. I decided that I would just get it over with and tell Black. I couldn't wait to hear what he'd have to say. I dialed his number before I pulled out of the parking spot.

"What's up?" he said into the phone. He sounded like he wasn't in such a good mood, which might have been even better. I should be able to brighten up his day with this news.

"You don't sound too happy to hear from me, what's up?"

"I just got a lot of shit on my mind that's all. What's up?"

"Well, I have some good news."

"What's that?" he said blandly. This wasn't going to be as easy as I thought. Whatever was on his mind must have been really bothering him.

"We're having a baby," I said, excited. He didn't respond. That definitely wasn't the reaction I was hoping for. "Did you hear me, I said we're having a baby."

"I'm going to call you back in a little while. I have to handle something."

Click!

What the hell? I thought. Did he just hang up on me or was my mind playing tricks on me? He didn't just do that. I stared at the phone hoping that it would ring again. I felt like bursting into tears. Was all that I've done in vain? I felt like a damn fool. I couldn't even think straight. I was hyperventilat-

ing at one point. I'd gotten so worked up I had to pull over. I
mean, I was at the point of no return. What could I do if he
didn't want this baby or if he didn't want me? That wasn't an
option. Maybe I was overreacting and something really important caused him to end the call so abruptly. I sat there in the
car for the next ten minutes before I calmed down enough
to maneuver through traffic safely. I made it home and was
still out of sorts when I got there. I slammed the door and
stomped my feet up to the room like a twelve-year-old. Now
been holding on to it until the right time and what better been
holding on to it until the right time and what better almost
forty-five minutes since he hung up on me. I wouldn't give
in and call him again. I wasn't a weak chick, I wasn't even an
emotional chick so I didn't know where the hell all of it was
coming from. Wait, yes I did, this damn baby was taking me
over. I got up to the bedroom and lay across the bed. I was
exhausted and I hoped that maybe if I took a nap by the time
I got up he'd be here apologizing for dissing me.

Chapter 14

Black

Take This Ring

I sat there staring at the phone and feeling like the biggest asshole on the planet. Did she just say we were having a baby? How the hell did that happen? I wasn't ready for that. Not that I don't love kids but with so much shit going on it wasn't the time to bring a baby into the world. Shit, I still had to look over my shoulder every time I took a step to make sure someone wasn't sneaking up on me. I knew she'd be pissed but even more hurt the way that I reacted but at the time I couldn't think of anything else to say. I figured not saying anything at all was better than saying the wrong thing. If she was pregnant and planned on keeping it, there wasn't anything that I could say to change her mind. With Diamond that was virtually impossible. Now, I not only had to worry about keeping her safe but a baby as well. And what would Trice do? That was a whole different issue in itself. I could see her becoming more conniving once she got a whiff of the news. JB sat across from me trying to figure out what the hell was going on. His lips were moving but I could no longer hear him.

"Hello, is anybody in there?" JB said, waving his hands in front of my face trying to break my stare.

"Yeah I'm here," I said shaking out of it for a second.

"Yo', what happened? Who was that on the phone?"

"That was Diamond, I just did some dumb shit."

"What? I was sitting right here and I didn't hear you say anything but you'll call her back."

"Yeah, that's the problem, I didn't say anything. She just told me that she was pregnant and I hung up on her."

He sat back in his chair with a puzzled look on his face. "Damn, that's heavy."

"Tell me about it. I didn't mean to diss her like that, she just caught me off guard. Now I feel like shit because it came across like I don't want it and it's not even like that."

"Well, call her back and explain it. That should settle it, right?"

"Man, that shit ain't going to just go away like that. You don't know her like I do and she's not that easy to smooth over when shit gets rough."

"I don't know what else to tell you, can't say buy her some shit 'cause she can buy anything her damn self."

"Let me show you something," I said as I opened up the drawer and removed the black velvet ring box that I'd locked up inside. I sat it on the desk in front of him without opening it.

"Is that what I think it is?" He asked with a surprised look on his face.

"Yeah it is, open it."

He sat up and grabbed the box off the desk and opened it. "Damn man, this shit is tight. Why didn't you give it to her?"

"Because it didn't make sense. We still haven't straightened out this shit with Kemp that's lingering on and realistically she couldn't marry me if she's still married to him."

"So you really believe he's still alive?"

"I don't know what to believe anymore. I do know someone is out there trying to kill me."

"I mean, we were both at the funeral. I know damn well I saw them put his body in the ground. Unless he has a twin, he's dead. I think someone is trying to fuck with you and by the looks of it they're succeeding. You can't let this shit put your life on hold. If you love her, marry her. She's having your seed now too—you have to keep it moving."

What he said made total sense. Here I was tripping about a nigga that I knew for a fact was dead. This whole situation had gotten out of hand and the more I let it get to me the worse things got between me and Diamond. He was right, that's exactly what they wanted to do. Fuck it, I was going to give her the ring and I was going to do it tonight. I wasn't waiting around any longer.

"You're absolutely right," I said, laughing. "Why am I tripping, I know what needs to be done."

"What about the baby?"

"I'm actually excited about that, believe it or not."

"Well, congrats then, nigga," he said, standing up to give me dap. I grabbed the box back off the table and instead of tucking it back inside the drawer I put it in my pocket. I'd been holding on to it until the right time and what better time then the present.

"So a quick change in subject, I talked to Money and he's going to get with you sometime this week. We're moving forward with this partnership."

"Word, I'm glad you thought it over. I trust him, he's a good dude."

"Well, if not, I'll have you to blame for it." I said, sternly. Though JB and me were cool, business was business and if for any reason this nigga Money fucked me over, I'd be on his ass. He looked at me as if he wasn't expecting it.

"Why you coming at me like that? You know I'd take him out my damn self if anything shiesty comes up," he said, putting his hand on his chest.

"I'm not coming at you, I'm just saying, you brought him to my attention so if something happens it's partly your fault."

"I'll accept that but I gotta run, I have a few stops to make. I'll get with you later." He reached over to shake my hand.

"Okay, cool." I replied, as I extended my arm to shake his hand.

Once he left the room I dialed Diamond. Surprisingly she didn't pick up. I thought for sure she'd at least answer and curse me out. I didn't bother to leave a message, I just headed home to straighten this out. As I pulled up to the house and turned into the driveway a blue Camry quickly sped off from the opposite side of the street. Normally I wouldn't pay something like that any mind but they peeled off so damn fast they left tire marks in the street. Plus, with all of the shit that had been going down lately I had to be extremely careful and pay close attention to my surroundings. If I didn't, that would definitely give them the advantage and I wasn't going to go that route.

I got up to the door and opened it. It was pretty quiet but I knew she was home because her car was in the driveway.

"Diamond," I yelled out through the house. I didn't get an answer so I thought she might have been asleep. I walked into the bedroom and saw her stretched out across the bed.

She looked peaceful but as I walked closer I could see the dry tear tracks on both sides of her face. Seeing the evidence of her tears made feel even worse than I had before I got there. I stood there holding onto my pocket wondering if it was the right time to pop the question. I wasn't sure if I was ready and now that I was standing there I was more nervous than I would have imagined I'd be at this point in my life. I stood there for a few more minutes almost afraid to wake her. She must have felt my presence because she woke up and noticed me before I was able to leave the room.

"Hey babe, I didn't mean to wake you." I turned to face her. She didn't respond, only getting up from the bed and heading into the bathroom.

"Diamond, can we talk?"

She stopped in her tracks and turned to walk back to the door. "Talk about what? How you just dissed me? I told you I was having your baby and you hung the phone up!" she yelled as she paced back and forth. She had every reason to be upset.

"I'm sorry, okay, it just caught me off guard and I wasn't dissing you, I would never do that to you."

"Maybe you didn't want to but that's exactly what you did. That shit was low for you, I never thought you wouldn't be able to take care of your responsibility."

"I can take care of my responsibility. It's not about that, it's really about nothing. I said I was sorry."

She stood there staring as if there was something that she wanted to say but couldn't. She shook her head and turned to continue her trip into the bathroom.

"Diamond," I called out to her.

"What?" she yelled with her back still facing me.

"Could you turn around, please? I need to show you something." I pulled the ring box from my pocket and opened it.

She turned and looked at me, still angry. Not immediately noticing the ring, she said, "What is it Black, I'm really not in the mood for . . ." She was now staring at the box in my hand. Her frown quickly turned into a smile and tears soon followed that smile. "Are you serious?"

"Dead serious," I said as I walked over to where she was standing. Diamond was never the mushy type and now that I knew she was pregnant that said it all. The mood swings and the arguments—I mean, it was all out of character for her. Honestly, some of it I could get used to. Assuming how she felt was what I'd done in the past—knowing sure felt a lot better. I guess this pregnancy had its pros and cons after all. I removed the ring from the small velvet box and placed it on her finger as she held out her hand for me. Tears were still flowing as she moved in and kissed me.

"I'm sorry I'm so emotional, this isn't me. I love you so much, I'm happier than you know." She hugged me.

I felt good, and I hoped that the feeling would last. In the past, I've been known for losing interest in women after a while but I didn't see that happening with her. Regardless of the ups and downs she was actually one of the only women I felt this strong of a connection to. After a few seconds the smile that brightened her face became dim.

"What's wrong?"

"I'm just thinking about Kemp—we can't get married if he's still alive."

"Look, I honestly don't believe that it's Kemp. Someone else has to know what happened and just wants to fuck with us. I think I know him more than anyone and if he really wanted us dead, trust me, we would have been dead by now. That's real talk, D, I don't see it, I just don't." I shook my head.

"How would someone know what happened? I would have been in jail by now if that was the case."

"Obviously they want something from us, I just have to find out what the hell it is."

"I'm just scared, with the baby coming and all, I don't want anything to happen."

"It won't, trust me, you've believed in me this long, don't stop now. I'm not going to let anything happen to you. I promise." I reached out to hug her and she obliged, wrapping her arms tightly around me.

I had to find out who it was and I had to find out sooner than later. I wasn't about to let this shit ruin my future. The business was being affected as well and I couldn't have that either. The workers were turning against me, niggas were stealing money, and people didn't fear me in the streets. I'd worked too hard and too long to let shit slip away now.

Chapter 15

Diamond

Knock You Down

There was a loud knock at the door. I never liked the sound of that in the wee hours of the morning. I glanced to the left and the time on the alarm clock read three-thirty. Black still hadn't made it home yet. I figured that out when I felt the untouched spot next to me in bed. I got up and grabbed my robe from the back of the bedroom door before going downstairs. As I neared the door the knocks got louder. It was raining out too and the sound of the water beating against the windows didn't even muffle their knocking.

"Who is it?" I yelled, hoping that they'd stop.

"Ma'am, it's the police. We need you to open the door, please."

"The police?" I looked through the peephole and saw two male officers standing outside. One was black and the other was white. I slowly unlocked the door and opened it. "Can I help you?"

"Yes, we're looking for Diamond Brooks, is that you?" the black officer said immediately.

"Yes, that is me, my last name isn't Brooks anymore but how can I help you?"

"We need to take you down to the station for questioning. I need you to go get dressed."

"Questioning? At three o'clock in the morning? What do you have to question me about?"

"The death of your deceased husband and one Mica Thompson."

"What? Why would you need to question me now—that happened over a year ago." My heart dropped to my stomach. What the hell was going on?

"Please ma'am, just get dressed so we can take care of this."

"What if I say no?"

"You don't have a choice, we can come back with a warrant if you'd like," the white cop added.

I was pissed and I was afraid. I couldn't go back to jail. I was pregnant. I wasn't about to have my baby behind bars. The officers were pretty clear so I knew that the only option I had was to go along with it. I motioned with my hands to allow them in from the rain. They came in and stood near the door as I headed upstairs to throw something on. I was afraid to call Black since they were probably standing downstairs listening. Instead I sent a text message to his phone explaining what was going on. I hurried into a sweat suit and sneakers and ran back downstairs. I followed them out of the door and into the police car that was waiting at the end of the driveway. My heart was pounding and my entire body was trembling. I didn't know what was going to happen to me at this point but whatever it was it couldn't have been good. It took us about fifteen minutes to reach the station. Once inside they placed me in a room alone. The room was cold and small. The walls were painted dark gray with white around the edges. There was a small wooden table in the center of the room with one chair on each side. There was also a large mirror on the wall opposite the table, which I assumed they could view me from the other side. I tried to keep my cool and not look all nervous because I was sure I was being watched. If I looked guilty they'd be sure to use it against when they had the opportunity.

Twenty minutes a plainclothes white detective entered the room. He looked to be in his late fifties, early sixties. His hair was mixed with gray and he was dressed in black dress pants and a white button-down shirt. He had a smirk on his face that rubbed me the wrong way. I still remained calm.

"Hello, Ms. Brooks. Is it okay if I call you Diamond?"

"That's fine," I said, blandly.

"Okay Diamond, my name is Detective Hill."

I sat silent.

"I'm sure you want to get down to business so I won't keep you waiting any longer. We've recently gotten some information that indicates you as a suspect in the murder of your husband and one Mica Thompson." He sat down in the chair opposite me.

"That's ludicrous, I didn't have anything to do with that. It was a home invasion and robbery, everyone knows that."

"Well, we have a witness that tells us otherwise."

"Well, your witness is mistaken. I wasn't even anywhere near the house when it happened. When I came home the cops were already at my house."

"I'm going to give it to you straight. They claim to have video that will back up their story even though we already have evidence to put you away as an accessory to murder."

"An accessory? You just said that they said I was the murderer."

"That's not what I said, I said that you were implicated in the murder. The charges are against your boyfriend, Black."

"What?" I yelled. Who the hell would try and put everything on him? He had nothing to do with it.

"What we believe happened is you walked in on the murder and you ended up covering for him."

"That's so far from the truth it doesn't even make sense." My heart was pounding even harder than it had been a few minutes earlier. "Where are you getting your information?" I asked as if he would really give me the answer to that question.

"That's confidential. The bottom line here is that if you choose not to tell us what happened, we'll lock you up right along with him."

"Neither him nor I had anything to do with it and that's the truth. I don't know why someone would tell you that. I loved my husband. I would have never hurt him and Black was his best friend."

"His best friend that you're now in a relationship with? That's extremely suspicious, especially when you inherited all that he had."

"I was his wife, who else was it supposed to go to?"

"I'm going to walk out of here and give you a few minutes to think, okay? I'm not going to sit here answering your questions and you haven't been able to answer any of mine."

"But . . ."

"There is no but, you need to talk or you're going to jail."

"Well in that case, I need to call my lawyer," I replied. I knew that they didn't have anything concrete because my ass would have been in a cell rather than sitting here doing a damn survey.

"I figured you'd say that, that's what all criminals say!" he said as he walked out and closed the door behind him.

I was pissed. What the fuck did he mean by that? Okay, I know that I was the one that committed the murder and I couldn't let Black go down for that. I had to somehow let him know what was going on. I was praying that he hadn't rushed down here to the station like I'd asked in the text because they'd probably never let him go. I didn't know what to do but I knew that I had to get my lawyer on this if I wanted to walk out of here. After a few more minutes of waiting, they took me out to the desk so that I could call my lawyer. After I called and left her a voicemail they took me right back into the box that I'd been in for the past two hours. Black had to have been worried sick and I refused to call him. Then I thought about it—Kiki. I could call Kiki so that she could somehow get a message to him. Just as I was about to sit down I told him that I had figured out who I wanted to call. The officer looked at me as if I'd pissed him off but I didn't give a damn, I needed to make my phone call.

The phone rang a few times before she picked up. "Hey Kiki, it's D, I need you to do me a favor."

"Girl, what the hell do you need me to do at five in the morning."

"I'm down at the police station, girl, they . . ." I turned to look at the officer who was standing behind me. I gave him a look like *Damn can I get a little privacy* and he sighed as he turned his attention toward the other things going on around the precinct. "The cops came to the door this morning saying they have a witness that fingers Black as the one who killed Kemp and Mica."

"What?" she yelled. "Who the hell is the witness?"

"I don't know but I need you to get a message out for me, I can't really say because they're watching me like a hawk but I'm sure you know what I mean."

"I got you, Diamond, don't worry, girl, everything will work itself out."

"Thanks Kiki, I love you, girl."

"I love you too."

I hung up and was then walked back into the interrogation room. I was tired, cold, and annoyed. I kept my fingers crossed and hoped that this would all go away as some type of misunderstanding. I had to figure out how to get myself out of this one. I waited and the longer it took for them to return the angrier I got. I heard the doorknob turning and prepared myself for the worst.

"So, have you thought it over?" the detective asked with a smirk on his face.

"Look, where's my lawyer? I'm not talking to you anymore until she shows up."

Just then Ms. Baker, my lawyer, walked through the door. I instantly felt a little bit of weight being lifted off of my shoulders.

"Sorry it took me so long to get here," she said as she walked around to the side of the table where I was seated. "What are you charging my client with?"

"She's been fingered as an accessory to two murders."

"Fingered? So I assume that means you haven't pressed charges yet?"

"Not officially, but we will very soon."

"Well, then we're finished here. Diamond, come on, you're free to go."

"Just like that?" I asked, shocked.

"Just like that!" she replied as she headed toward the door and motioned for me to follow.

I jumped up out of that chair faster than a cheetah. I wish I would have known I could have left because I would have done that hours earlier. I turned and looked back and gave the detective the same smirk that he had been giving me each time he'd walked into the room. He gave me a look that said a thousand words. Like this wasn't over and I wasn't going to get over that easy. I walked out of there and Ms. Baker offered me a ride home. I knew that she'd pick my brain on the way.

"Now, what's going on here, Diamond?"

"They are accusing me of being an accomplice to the murder of my husband and my best friend. They're saying that Black was the one that murdered them. There isn't any truth to that whatsoever but they claim that they have a witness."

"Witnesses can be broken so don't worry yourself too much about that. Have you spoken to Black?"

"No, I didn't want to call him and risk him being dragged down there with me."

"Good, well believe this, if their witness was as strong as they claim they are, you'd both be locked up. They haven't arrested you yet because they don't have enough evidence."

"Thank you so much for getting down there. I know it was before business hours."

"Don't worry about that, Diamond, I work for you and believe me, you'll get through this, I'll make sure of it."

By then we were pulling up in front of my house. I got out and waved good-bye. I hadn't even made it up to the steps before Black was coming out of the front door.

"Babe, what the hell happened?"

"The cops came and knocked on the door saying that they needed to take me down to the station for questioning and then when I got there they were saying that they have a witness that is fingering both you and me for Kemp and Mica's murder."

"What? A witness? How the hell could they have a witness?"

"I don't know, but it probably has something to do with the person who's been terrorizing us."

"What did Ms. Baker say?"

"She said that their case must not be strong or else both of us would be in jail. She says not to worry about it."

"Not to worry? Someone is trying to put us under and I'm not going to rest until I find out who the fuck it is!"

"Babe, don't go out there and get hurt. Please don't do anything crazy—we have a baby on the way."

"I know that, but these muthafuckers are taking me for a joke. I'm not about to get knocked down and not get the fuck back up. This shit is getting way out of hand."

"I'm just afraid, I'm not trying to have this baby behind bars."

"You're not going to. Look, if no one else understands, I do. I know why you did what you did and I never bashed you for it. Yeah, Kemp was my friend but all is fair in love and war. Shit happens and if you hadn't shot him when you did, trust me, someone else would have."

I stood there silent. I hadn't even made it into the living room. I was still standing near the door. My heart was pounding. I couldn't relax and I was beginning to feel sick to my stomach. My head was spinning and it was becoming hard to breathe. "I need to sit down, babe, I feel like I'm about to faint," I said, placing one hand on my forehead.

"Come on," he said, grabbing my hand and leading me over to the sofa. "You have to calm down. You can't let this wear you out."

I had reached the sofa and sat down but I was still feeling sick. "Babe, I feel like I'm . . ." I threw up right on him and all over the sofa and the floor. He didn't even budge; he sat there next to me with his hand gently rubbing across the top of my back. "I'm so sorry, I didn't have enough time to warn you."

"It's okay come on, let's go upstairs so you can lie down and rest. I'll clean this up in a little while."

I agreed and got up from the sofa and followed him upstairs. My nerves had gotten the best of me. Once I got up to the bedroom I went into the master bathroom to wash the throw-up off of me. My shirt was soaked and the smell of it almost made me do it again. I sat down on the side of the tub and put my face in the palms of my hands. What the hell had I gotten myself into? If I thought things were bad in the past they were definitely only going to get worse.

Chapter 16

Black

Falling

"What the hell do you expect me to do, just wait around and let them lock my ass up for some shit that I had nothing to do with?" I yelled at JB. I didn't normally take my anger out on him but he was pissing me off.

"That's not what I'm saying, I'm just saying the way that you are approaching the situation is only going to make things worse."

"Well, this is the only way I know how to handle shit and if I have to keep shooting mothafuckers until somebody tells me who the fuck the culprit is that's what I'm going to do. Nigga, I got kids and a woman to think about."

"I know, but . . ."

"But what? There is no *but*; you said that you would ride for me and you had my back—now that's what the fuck I need from you."

JB sat across from me with a frown on his face. No man likes to be spoken to like a child, but hell, he wasn't getting the point. I was angry, but I knew if I had to go around town putting a gun to people's head for information I would. This shit was stressing me because I couldn't go to jail—I had too much shit to live for. Money entered the room a few seconds later and he must've felt the heat in the room.

"Damn, is everything cool?" he asked, barely shutting the door before he spoke.

"Hell no, everything ain't cool, someone is out here trying to sabotage me and I'm not having that shit."

"Well, anything you need me to do, I'm here. It ain't even going down that easy."

I could see sweat building up on JB's forehead. Money and I had gotten close since this partnership and slowly but surely JB was taking his self out of the equation. All of that *you're like my brother and I wouldn't let anything happen to you* shit wasn't much more than words and it was just making me angry in times like these. Money had been stepping up to the plate the past few weeks and I respected that. JB continued to give him a stare of death while I continued to pace back and forth.

"Look, I'll put every nigga that run with me on it for you. We're going to find out who it is, I put my life on that."

I stopped in my tracks and turned to look at him. "Thanks man, I really appreciate that shit." I stuck out my hand to give him dap and he obliged.

"It's no problem. You've looked out for me that's the least I can do. I'm going to get on that right now and I'll keep you updated."

"Cool, thanks again."

He walked out and even though I felt a little better knowing that niggas had my back I still continued to pace across the floor. It was quiet except for the sounds my boots were making on the floor. Without that you could hear a pin drop.

"Yo' I know you're going through it right now but you have to use your head on this one. I'm starting not to trust this nigga Money. I mean he just met you a few months ago and he's ready to ride for you like he's known you his whole life. I don't like that shit."

"Why, because you ain't doing the same thing? Don't hate on him now when you're the one that was on his dick from jump," I yelled.

"On his dick? I wasn't on his dick, I just saw an opportunity that's made you more money."

"Me? Nigga, it made *us* more money, not just me."

"Look, I'm going to let you calm down a little. I know how shit feels when the walls are closing in but you know I ain't going to let shit happen to you. I just think that once you calm down and think about the shit a lot of the moves you want to make now won't seem so smart."

Maybe he was right, maybe I did need some time to calm down. Maybe I needed to get away for a little while to ease my mind. I didn't know who to trust and which way to turn. I had to protect what was mine and that included my family.

"I'm going to take a trip for a few days, you think you and Tommy can handle things until I get back?"

"Of course, man, I think that's a good idea. A few days away from this drama will do your mind good, I guarantee that."

"All right, I'm going to bounce and get home to check on D. I'll probably ride out tomorrow or Friday."

"All right, let me know if you need anything."

"All right." I said before he got up to leave the office. I left out shortly after that to go home and check on Diamond. I had two workers sitting outside of the house to make sure she was safe. I pulled up in front and gave both of them a nod. I went in the house where Diamond was laying on the sofa watching TV.

"Hey babe, what brings you home so early?" she said, sitting up.

"I wanted to come and check on you plus I wanted to tell you to pack a bag so we can go to Vegas tomorrow."

"Vegas? Tomorrow, why?"

"Because I need to get away from all of this bullshit for a few days. I need to make some precise moves and dealing with all of this is clouding my mind."

"Well, who's going to run everything while we're gone? We can't trust everyone to keep things in order."

"We're only going a few days and I think that it will be good for both of us. You could use a vacation too."

"Yeah, you're probably right," she said with a slight smile.

"Plus we can get married too if you want," I said in a low tone. I thought that she might not have heard me but she definitely did.

"Are you serious? I would love to but I don't want you to rush into it because of everything that's going on now."

"I'm not rushing, I know where my heart is and I know that's what will make you happy."

"Well, I'm down then, nigga!" she said, bursting into laughter. We both laughed together and for a moment we forgot about all of the drama.

"I have to go back out but I just wanted to check on you. Do you need anything before I go?"

"No, I'm cool, I'll start getting my stuff together now. I'm excited, I've never been to Vegas before." She laughed.

"Okay," I said as I laughed with her. I gave her a hug before I was on my way back out the door. Just as I began to back out the driveway two police cars pulled up behind me with flashing lights and sirens blaring.

"Turn off your vehicle and step out of the car with your hands in the air," one of the police officers yelled as he stood with his door open and his gun in hand.

I got out of the car with my hands up as he'd requested. I was pissed though I knew what this was about. I knew that they'd come for me sooner or later. Diamond came running out of the house yelling.

"What are you doing? He didn't do anything," she cried.

"Stop right there, ma'am," the officer from the other vehicle yelled.

I looked around and the two workers were standing outside of the car most likely waiting on a signal from me. I gave them a look that kept them calm.

"Diamond, listen to them, please. Call the lawyer and tell her to meet me down at the station. Don't worry, babe, they don't have anything to hold me on."

The officer had handcuffed me and began walking toward the car and reading me my rights. I'd heard those rights before in the past but I still couldn't get used to it. Diamond was standing at the top of the steps as the officer got in the car and began to drive down the street. She still had tears streaming down her face. Even though I wasn't the one that murdered them I'd take the rap for it rather than have her locked away. I cared about her too much. Once we reached the station I was thrown into a holding cell, a small-ass box with a metal door and a small window, I felt like I was suffocating it was so damn hot in there. I sat down on the metal bench and leaned my head up against the wall. I prayed that my lawyer would get here fast and straighten everything out.

Chapter 17

Diamond

For You I Will

It was time for his arraignment and Ms. Baker was confident that she could get him off. I was standing outside of the courtroom pacing. Ms. Baker met me in the hall where I stood nervous and feeling sick but I was going to hold it together until this was all over with.

"Stop worrying so much, it's going to be okay," she said, placing her hand on my shoulder. "Let's go head inside; they should be bringing him out shortly."

"Okay," I replied as I followed behind her.

The courtroom was packed with people. I remembered this all too well since I'd been in the same position just a few years ago myself. I found a seat and waited patiently, though my nerves were shot. When I saw him walking out with the officer behind him I smiled. I was so happy to see him even in these circumstances. I wished that I could hug him—my body had been yearning for his touch. He looked around the room as if he was trying to see if I was there. I stood up just before he turned around and blew him a kiss. He smiled and sat down.

"The Honorable Herbert Johnson, judge presiding. Please be seated and come to order," the clerk, said, standing over to the side of the bench.

"Good afternoon, ladies and gentlemen. In the matter of the people of the State of Pennsylvania versus Keshawn Black. Counsel, your appearances please," the Judge said loudly as he took his seat on the bench.

"Good afternoon, Your Honor, Rob Spencer and John Wilks on behalf of the people," the district attorney said, standing.

"Your Honor, good afternoon. Trisha Baker, attorney on behalf of Keshawn Black, who's present in custody before the court."

"All right, and with you?"

"Your Honor, this is Mr. Joseph Rake, an investigator, who will be assisting in the case."

"All right. Mr. Spencer, are you ready to proceed in this arraignment matter?"

"Yes, Your Honor. At this time the people would file, with this court, a ten-count complaint against defendant Keshawn Black, date of birth, February 8, 1975. The people are filing five counts, one of them murder, the first count charges the defendant with murder with gun allegations pursuant to 12022.53, as well as special circumstances pursuant to penal code 190.2. The remaining counts are four counts of attempted murder, premeditated attempted murder, all with the gun allegations, again pursuant to penal code section 12022.53. The remaining counts are assault with a firearm charges, again with the attendant gun allegations. We are filing this complaint in this court due to the fact that the defendant personally killed the victim in these crimes."

"Mr. Black, how do you plead?" The judge turned to look over at Black.

"Not guilty," he responded.

"Okay, Mr. Black, to your plea as the court has recorded them, not guilty to all of the counts in the indictment," the clerk said.

"Thank you and you may be seated Mr. Black," the judge instructed. "Now, due to the severity of the charges here, there will be no bail set."

"Judge, my client is a respected business owner and is not a flight risk. I ask that some sort of bail be made for my client."

"The charges are A felonies, Ms. Baker,.I'm sure you are aware how dangerous that would be to allow him to remain free during trial preparation and trial."

"Judge, my client is not a danger to society and we will prove that the charges against my client are bogus. The state claims to have one witness and no solid evidence."

"Is this true, counsel?" the judge asked, turning toward the district attorney.

"We do have one witness, Your Honor—it's actually one of the victims, Mica Thompson. We have her testimony that Mr. Keshawn Black shot both her and Lolan Kemp on the evening in question here. She's actually present here today."

My heart dropped to the floor. Black looked back at me and as I was looking around I spotted Mica off to the left side of the courtroom. She'd survived. Then I thought back to that day when I swore I saw her driving by me. How did this happen? Why would she accuse Black and not me? Black looked shocked as if he'd seen a ghost. She looked over at me with a look that could kill. We were staring each other down like we were about to go to war. Then she gave a devilish grin and sat back down.

"Ms. Baker, my decision stands, there will be no bail set at this time. We will revisit it later as we get closer to trial."

"Thank you, Judge," she said as she sat back down.

"So that's it, I'm going to be stuck in jail?" Black said in anger as he turned to Ms. Baker. "I didn't have anything to do with this."

"I know, Black, but there isn't anything that we can do at this time. We will talk later, okay?"

Black was pissed and I could see the anger in his face as the officer grabbed him by the arm so he could stand and be escorted out of the courtroom. I silently cried as they took him away. What the hell was I supposed to do now? Ms. Baker and her assistant walked toward me and motioned for me to come with her.

"What is going on? He can't stay in jail, I need him," I said as soon as we were outside the door.

"I told you to trust me, he's not going to be there very long. Just give me some time to straighten things out."

"I can't believe this. I . . ." I stopped in my tracks as Mica walked out of the courtroom. I wanted to say something but I couldn't find the words to speak. She slowly walked toward Ms. Baker and me.

"Well, well, well. If it isn't Ms. Diamond Diva. Long time no see, congrats on the baby. Too bad you're going to be a single parent."

"Don't respond," Ms. Baker jumped in.

"I'm not because she's not worth it."

"Tell that to your man when he gets locked away for the rest of his life!" She yelled.

"You know what, Mica, you're going to get what you deserve, believe that."

"Is that a threat? Because if it is, I'll have you locked up right along with him."

"Diamond, come on, let's go."

Mica laughed loudly as we headed toward the door. I turned to look back at her before making it through and she was still laughing. She took her hands as if she had a gun and pointed it at me while still laughing. I turned around and walked out of the door. I was furious. I got in my car and picked up my cell to dial Kiki. My hands were shaking and I felt like I was going to lose everything I had, including Black.

"Hello," Kiki said in a low tone.

"Mica is alive," I yelled.

"What?"

"She's alive, she was in court today. She's the witness that they have. Black is going to go to jail for what I did. What am I going to do, Kiki?"

"What do you mean, she's alive? They had a funeral for her and everything."

"It was a memorial. Damn, Kiki, how did this happen?"

"I don't know D, do you think that she had something to do with all of the stuff that's been happening to you and Black?"

"You know what, now it all makes sense—it has to be her. I knew I wasn't crazy. Kemp is dead—it's been her all the time. Someone has to be working with her, I can't see her doing all of that on her own."

"Who do you think would be helping her?"

"I don't know, but that's what I am going to figure out. I'm not going to just sit back and let Black rot in jail. If I have to kill that bitch, I will, and this time I won't make the mistake of not checking her pulse," I yelled in frustration. "I have to call JB and tell him what's going on. I'll call you back, Kiki."

I hung up.

Instead of calling I decided to drive down to the warehouse. When I pulled up a few workers were standing outside. They all turned to look at me at the same time. Probably all anxious to see what was going on with Black.

"Hey D, how did everything go at court?" Tommy was the first one to speak.

"Not good, not good at all. Is JB here?"

"Yeah, he's inside. Is there anything that you need us to do?" Money stepped up and asked. I didn't even know him that well but I didn't get a good vibe from him. I felt like he was up to something from the moment that Black introduced me to him.

"No, I'm fine," I replied as I opened the door to go inside. JB was sitting in Black's office on the phone. He was quite comfortable with his feet on the desk and his chair leaning back. He jumped up as soon as he noticed me and quickly ended his call. I didn't know who to trust, but Black told me if anything ever happened, JB was the only one I should talk to.

"What happened down at court?" he asked as soon as he ended his call.

"They kept him and they wouldn't give him a bail."

"Why not?"

"Because Mica is alive and she's saying that he's the one that shot her and Kemp."

"Wait a minute, she's alive?"

"Yes, I think she has something to with all of the shit that happened. The fire, the car bomb, all of it."

"Are you serious?"

I gave him a look that said it all. I wished that I wasn't serious. I wished that it was all a dream that I would wake up from.

"Well, what do you need me to do? Whatever it is, I'll handle it."

"I need you to find out who's helping her and I need her ass eliminated. Without her they have no case. If she's dead they'll have to let Black out." I meant every word of that. I was going to do whatever I had to do for him. I had to because I knew that he'd stay there if it meant keeping me out. We not being together just wasn't an option.

"Okay, don't worry about it, I'll take care of everything for you."

"Thanks, JB, I really appreciate it. He's gonna need you to continue taking care of things out here until he gets out."

"No doubt, I got it."

"Okay," I said as I headed back out to the car. Money walked over to me just as I was about to get in.

"Hey Diamond, I'm sorry about Black. I just want you to know that if you need anything—I mean anything—I'm here for you." He reached his hand out and touched mine. I quickly pulled my hand away.

"Thanks, Money, I'll keep that in mind." I tried not to be rude but I hoped that he wasn't coming on to me.

"Okay, well, I won't hold you. Here's my number, make sure you use it."

I didn't even respond as he gave me a devilish grin and

began to walk away. Black would kill him if he even thought he was looking at me too hard. That wasn't the first time that he'd said or done something that I didn't feel too comfortable with but I still hadn't told Black. I was too focused on getting him out of jail. I got in the car and saw through the rearview mirror that he was still standing there as I drove away. The drive home seemed especially long because so much was going through my mind. I pulled up to the house probably in about twenty minutes but it felt like an hour. I parked, got out, and walked up to the door. Just as I turned the knob someone called my name.

"Diamond," a female voice yelled.

I turned around to find Trice standing there with her and Black's son holding her hand. What the hell did she want? I thought.

"Yeah," I replied.

"Look, I know I don't know you but since Black's been locked up I've been struggling and since you're his girl you have access to his money. I need some money for his son."

"I'm sorry you've been struggling but I don't have access to his money, so I can't help you."

"I'm trying to be nice here. You don't know how hard it was for me to come here today. When I found out you were with him I was furious and then when I found out you were pregnant I hated you. Then I felt like an ass for it. I don't know you but I know Black and regardless of the badass street persona he's a good dude and if he loves you then I can't hate you. I'm really just asking for some help—whatever you could do would help me."

She was melting my heart. How could I not help her and

the little boy who looked just like the man that I loved? This pregnancy was definitely changing me because if she'd said these same words to me before I was pregnant this conversation would have gone a whole lot different. If I turned her away I'd be the bitch that I used to be and the bitch that only cared about getting to the top and being in charge. I wasn't that person anymore and I honestly liked this person a lot better. I stood there quiet, trying to take it all in. I must've stood for a minute too long because she turned around and began to walk away.

"Trice," I called out to her. "Come in, let's sit down and talk. Let me know what you need and I'll make sure you get it."

"Thank you so much," she said, turning around and walking toward me. She followed me in to the house. I stood at the door for a second looking at the sky before I closed the door. Maybe this good deed would help things go right for me. At least that's what I hoped anyway.

Chapter 18

Diamond

Emergency

Two months had passed since the day of Black's arraignment and I still hadn't heard any news of him getting out. JB had been unsuccessful in finding Mica because they'd obviously had her in a witness-protection program. I hadn't seen her again since that day in the courtroom and honestly I wasn't trying to. The next time I saw her I wanted it to be in a casket. I was just two months shy of giving birth to the baby and I couldn't wait to get back to myself. Lately, Trice and I had become pretty cool. Kiki hated the idea but, shit, Kiki hated anybody she thought would take her spot as my best friend. I didn't plan on being friends with her but shit happens. She was actually fun to hang around; I could see why Black cared about her. She reminded me of myself—well, the way I used to be.

I hadn't been to Gia's in two weeks and I was in desperate need of a touch-up. I didn't have an appointment as usual but Gia would always bump me to the front of the line, pissing all the other girls in the salon off. I pulled up in my freshly cleaned BMW and parked right in front. There were a few random people standing outside on the corner and I could tell before I got inside that it was packed. I walked in and headed to the back.

"Hey girl," Gia yelled as she normally did when she saw me. She immediately stopped curling the girl's hair in her chair to give me a hug. "Look at you, all prego, I never thought I'd see the day," she laughed.

"Yeah, tell me about it, girl, I can't wait until this is all over so I can get back to normal."

"What you getting done today?"

"The works, my hair is a damn mess." I laughed, pointing to my head.

"Well, you can go head in the back to the shampoo girl, I'll do you next."

"Okay, cool." I walked in the back where the shampoo bowls were. I sat down and waited for the girl to come over, which took a little too long but shit, I just jumped in front a bunch of chicks outside. I couldn't be so impatient. She walked over to me with a smirk on her face. This was a new shampoo girl who I had never seen before. I wanted to know what the hell she was smiling about but then I remembered my ass was big and pregnant.

"You're Black's girl, right?" she asked.

What the hell was she asking me that for? I didn't know this girl from a can of paint so I wanted to know what the hell her motives were. "Yeah, why?" I asked with a straight face. I wanted her to know that I wasn't one to play with.

"I just wanted to say that it's fucked-up how he's stuck in jail. I know how it is to have a man behind bars. My dude's been in jail for three years," she said in that ghetto tone that

I hated. What the hell was she saying? I mean, I knew what she said but I wasn't sure what her angle was. I didn't trust females too much anyway, especially ones like her. I knew that I had a lot of haters out here and I had to always be on point no matter where I was.

"So what are you saying?" I asked honestly. She gave me a stare, like she thought that I was trying to play her in some way. Shit, I was just asking a question.

"I'm just saying, keep your head up when times get hard."

"Times won't get hard for me. I'm pretty well off on my own."

"Oh, excuse me if I hit a soft spot. I was just making conversation. Shit, it's hard being a single mom no matter how much dough you got." She laughed as the other women at the other stations shook their heads, agreeing with her. This chick must have me confused.

"It's not a soft spot, sweetie, and this ain't no talk show so I'm not going to sit here and entertain you and the peanut gallery over there. I simply need my hair washed and a hot oil treatment. Thank you very much."

She put her hand on her hip and sucked her teeth. I didn't want to have to put her in her place like that but I didn't have a choice. None of these bitches were on my level. "Matter fact, I'll wait until Gia's done so she can wash me," I said, sitting up from the bowl. She looked at me one last time and rolled her eyes before going up to the front. I guess she didn't know I could have her ass fired right then but like she said times were hard and I wasn't trying to snatch food out of her baby's mouth. Gia came back a few minutes later and laughed.

"You always start trouble when you come in here, girl. You lucky I love you!"

"No, they lucky I love you 'cause I'd be tearing this shop up!" I laughed. I was dead, serious though. Back in the day I would have whipped her ass in here.

"So what's up with Kiki? She ain't been in here in a minute." she asked as she pulled me back toward the sink and turned the water on.

"She's good. She's busy running that bar but you know Kiki she won't be gone too long."

"I know, girl, I missed you too. Your ass then got knocked and you don't visit a bitch no more."

"No, that ain't it, I've just been super-busy. I got so much to catch you up on, girl. We're going to have to go out to dinner or something one day."

"Cool, because I got some shit to catch you up on too."

"I bet you do." I burst into laughter. Gia always keep up with the rumor mill. I could always come to her when I wanted to know what was going on in the streets. I was out of the shop about an hour later and on my way home. This baby kept me exhausted and I needed to take a power nap. It was hot as hell outside. It was mid-summer and I hated the heat. I was trying to hurry up and get in the house near the AC. My cell phone started to ring and I fished through my bag to grab it. The phone dropped on the floor of the passenger side. I went to grab it and before I could sit back up.

Boom! That was the last thing I heard before my body experienced a numbing pain. Glass was everywhere. I had been hit on the driver's side so hard that the air bag deployed. I could feel blood running down from my head to the side of my face. I felt a sharp pain coming from my stomach and fluid running down my legs. I yelled out for help. The driver from the other car was now standing outside of my car window on the phone with a 911 operator. I kept yelling out that I was pregnant. I didn't care about anything but the baby at the time and though I never had a baby before I knew that I was in labor. It was too early, I was two months away from my due date. I cried each time a contraction hit and the other driver kept saying how sorry he was and asking if I was okay.

The ambulance arrived and came to my car immediately. The female opened the door on the passenger side and put a brace around my neck. "How far are the contractions?" she asked.

"I don't know, they're really close, please don't let me lose my baby," I cried.

"Don't worry, we're going to get you out of here."

Fire rescue had arrived as well and were on the driver's side, trying to pry the door open. Each movement hurt as I continued to cry in agony. I kept crying over and over to save my baby. I'd done too much to have this baby and I'd changed so much from it. It couldn't all be over now. It just couldn't. They had me out of the car and into the ambulance faster than I'd expected. They placed an IV in my arm and checked all of my vital signs. I couldn't hold in my tears, I was falling apart. I couldn't even call Black to have him run to the hospital and be by my side. I begged for them to call my father. I needed him since I had no one else.

We reached the hospital and they immediately rushed me into the trauma room. There were hands everywhere. My clothes were being cut off from every angle. The whole room was in a commotion.

"Ma'am, what's your name?"

"Diamond," I replied.

"Do you know where you are?"

"At the hospital."

"Do you know what year it is?" the doctor asked as he held open my eyes and waved a flashlight across them.

"It's 2008."

"How far along are you?" he asked, continuing the survey that was getting on my nerves. I wanted to know if my baby was okay.

"I'm thirty-two weeks, is my baby going to be okay?" I cried.

"We're going to do everything that we can to make sure of that." They were putting ultrasound gel on my stomach and wrapping the monitors around it. I could hear my baby's heartbeat. That sound was music to my ears. "We're going to try and hydrate you, this is just some fluid to hopefully stop the contractions," he said as he hooked a bag of fluid up to the IV. "Where are you in pain?"

"My head hurts and my left knee, and besides the contractions my left side is really hurting."

"If we can't stop the contractions we're going to have to take you in for an emergency cesarean. We're giving you some steroids just in case. The steroids will help the baby's lungs and breathing."

Everything was a blur, I was in so much pain. I couldn't really think straight. I just prayed that it would all be over soon. The contractions were slowing down, which I assumed was a good sign. The number of people that were in room had been cut down drastically. There was someone cleaning out the gash on the side of my head and putting some sort of stitching in it. My leg was still throbbing in pain even with the pain medication they'd given me.

"Once she's done we're going to get you up to X-ray and take some pictures of your leg. We think your knee may have been shattered."

"I just want my baby to be okay," I replied. Even after all that had happened and all of the pain that I was in, I just wanted my baby. I couldn't bear losing her.

"We're doing our best, you just relax we're taking care of you now. Your parents are out in the waiting area. After we get your X-rays we'll bring them in so you can see them for a brief moment."

"Okay," I replied with a sigh of relief.

I was taken up to X-ray a few minutes later and brought back down to the emergency room where the doctor confirmed that I'd need knee surgery. All of this because I went to pick up a damn phone. I didn't even know who the hell had been calling. The pain medication was working wonders because I wasn't feeling any pain. I was happy to still hear the fast heartbeat of my baby. I was going to go into surgery the same day but they called Pam and my dad in to see me before they took me to the operating room.

"Are you okay? I was so scared when I got that call," my dad said, moving close to the bed so he could kiss me on the forehead.

"I'm so glad you came. I'm okay but I'm going to have surgery on my knee."

"Well, you can come stay with us when you come home. I'll stay home to take care of you," Pam said after reaching over to give me a hug,

"No, you don't have to go through the trouble, I'll be okay."

"Knee surgery takes time to heal. You're going to need help

and it's not any trouble; that's the least I can do. I owe it to you," she replied, rubbing her hand across mine.

"I'll think about it, I promise."

"Well, they won't let us stay but we'll be here waiting for you to come out of surgery." My dad bent down to kiss me again.

"Okay, I love you . . . both," I said with a smile. Pam looked back at me as if she wasn't expecting to hear those words. Honestly, I wasn't expecting to say them but she'd grown on me and she was actually stepping up to the plate and making up for lost time.

They left the room and I was soon being prepped for surgery. The nurse came in and wheeled me up to the operating room. She gave me a few shots of something in my IV that had me on cloud nine.

"Think of going somewhere nice, like Aruba, that's where I want to go," she said as she pushed the gurney next to the operating table. It was ice-cold in the room and there were a few people with blue gowns and caps on their heads. I felt my eyelids getting heavier by the second. I listened to the nurse and tried to think of Aruba—shit, anywhere was better than that emergency room.

Chapter 19

Diamond

A Piece of Me

I heard an unfamiliar sound and my throat felt like I'd swallowed sandpaper. I woke up and noticed that I was still in the hospital. The sound that I heard was the nurse pressing the buttons on the machine that was hooked up to the IV. I felt different, like something was missing. I didn't hear the heat monitor. The sound that comforted me, which was my baby's heartbeat, wasn't there anymore. I rubbed my hands across my stomach, which was flat. My huge baby bump was gone. I panicked.

"Where's my baby, what happened to my baby?" I cried, trying to sit up in bed.

"Calm down, Diamond, your baby's fine, she's in the newborn intensive-care unit. During the knee surgery you went into labor so the doctors had to do an emergency C-section. You're baby's fine, don't worry. She's premature but she's a fighter."

"I need to go see her, I need to see her," I continued to cry.

"You can't go right now, you have to keep that leg flat until tomorrow. But I knew you'd want to see her so I had the

nurses over there take this picture for you." She pulled a Pola-
roid photo out of her lab jacket pocket.

I held the photo in my hand. She was so small and beautiful. I rubbed my hands across the picture before picking it up
and kissing it. "I love you, baby, I can't wait to hold you in my
arms. Thank you so much for this."

"No problem, the number is written over there on the
white board. You can call anytime to check on her and this
red button here, you can press whenever you need anything."
She pointed to the cord that was wrapped around the arm of
the bed.

"Okay, I'm really thirsty. Can I have something to drink?"

"You can eat these ice cubes. You'll be able to drink in a
few more hours. Call me if you need anything, I'll be right out
at the desk." She began to walk away. "By the way, what's the
baby's name?"

"Dior, her name is Dior." I looked down at the picture
once more.

"That's beautiful," she replied before leaving the room.

I put my head back against the pillow and thanked God
that she was okay. I wished Black could be here to see her and
be the support system that I needed. I felt comfortable resting; I believed that she was in good hands. I closed my eyes
and was just about to drift off to sleep when I heard a knock
on the door.

"Come in," I yelled as loud as I could with all that I had
been through. Kiki burst into the door with a huge smile on
her face.

"Girl, I'm so glad to see you, I almost died when I heard
about the accident. They were about to lock my ass up in the

lobby because they wouldn't let me up to see you. How are you feeling?" She was talking a mile a minute. I was happy that she came though she had my head spinning with all that she was saying.

"I'm okay, look at a picture of the baby." I still held it in my hand. I didn't want to let it go even for her to see.

"She's beautiful, D, when are you going to get to see her?"

"Hopefully tomorrow, I just can't believe all of this happened. I was reaching for the damn phone girl and that car smacked right into my door. I was in so much pain I just kept hoping the baby was okay."

"I'm so glad you both are okay. I know we haven't talked much lately but how's things with Black, any news?"

"No, that bitch Mica is in a witness-protection program. I had JB trying to find her and he didn't have any luck getting close to her. I'm so angry, girl, because it's all my fault. Now shit's falling apart with him gone, these niggas don't respect me. Who respects a woman like a man and a pregnant one at that. I don't know what to do but I can't lose everything. I have to figure something out."

"Well, right now you have to focus on getting better. You can't be in here stressing about that shit. You have a little baby to worry about now. Black will take care of it, you know they can't hold him on some shit they have no evidence on. They're just buying time hoping that something will pop up. They have nothing and they won't find anything, so don't stress."

"It's easy to say that from the outside looking in—look what's happened. Me and my baby could have died today while he's in jail serving time for something that I did." I began to get upset just thinking about it.

"Let's change the subject because I need you to get some rest. I just had to see your face and tell you I love you. I'm here if you need anything," she said, coming closer to me on the bed. "Everything will work out, trust me." She smiled.

"Thanks Kiki, I love you too, girl."

"All right I'm going to run, I have to get down to the bar, but make sure you call me if you need anything."

"I will."

She bent down, kissed me on the forehead, and headed out of the room. Eventually I couldn't fight the pain medication and I was off to sleep. I woke up the next morning ready to get up to go over to the nursery. As soon as the morning nurse came in I asked what time I'd be able to go. She told me around lunchtime, which put a damper on my day. I was ready to go at that moment in pain and all but I listened. Lunchtime couldn't have come fast enough and though it took me tons of tears and pain to get from the bed into a wheelchair I held it together long enough to be wheeled over. Once I got there and the nurse took her out of the warmer and put her in my arms I let go of the emotions. I could admit that in the beginning my plan to get pregnant may have been for the wrong reasons but as time went on I knew that it was meant for me. I was meant to be a mother and the mother of Black's child. There wasn't any other explanation for the joy that I felt as I looked down at the four-pound replica of him in my arms. Everything was going to be okay, I finally believed that. She was a piece of me and she turned me into the woman that I always hoped I'd be.

Chapter 20

Diamond

Back on my Feet

"I see nothing can hold you down, looking like a diva even in a hospital bed." Money laughed as he walked through the door of the hospital room. He was carrying a huge bouquet of flowers and three get-well-soon balloons. I was still nervous around him and I still hadn't been able to put my finger on what it was about him that bothered me.

"Thanks, Money," I said with a smile.

He walked over and sat the flowers on the ledge of the window and let the balloons loose. He came over to the bed, grabbed my hand, and kissed the back of it. What the hell was he doing? I didn't get this guy at all. I slowly pulled my hand away but not fast enough to let him know how much it bothered me.

"You look a hell of a lot better than I thought you would—you look just as beautiful as you always do." He gave a devilish grin and sat down on the edge of my bed. There were four chairs in the small room and instead of sitting in one of them he had to sit up close and personal with me. I could admit that he was sexy but I couldn't let that affect me. I'd gotten myself wrapped up before doing the same exact thing.

"So what's going on out there, how's business?" I quickly changed the subject.

"Everything's good, everything's falling into place."

"That's good to hear, I was worried."

"I'm sure, but I ain't come here to talk about work."

"Well, what did you come here for?" I asked, both shocked and confused.

"I'm being straight up with you, your man's going to be in jail for a very long time, if not forever. What do you plan to do, be celibate?"

"No, because my man will be home very soon, I'm sure of that."

"What makes you so sure of that? They have his victim ready and willing to point him out. You live in a fairy tale if you think he can get off from that."

"Maybe I like fairy tales." I shot back. I was getting annoyed. I knew Black was coming home soon. I wasn't going to let anyone rain on my parade.

"That's cool too, but what about reality? I'm a nigga that can make you feel good all over. I can fuck you mentally and physically so good you'll forget all about him. You haven't had love the way I can give it."

Was he serious? Niggas weren't shit, they'd turn on their partners in a heartbeat. He didn't crack a smile the entire time.

"I've been through this before—with Black, as a matter of fact. I can't let temptation ruin what I have with him."

"Temptation, huh? So I guess that means you're tempted to get some of this reality?"

"I didn't say that, I just said that I've been in a similar situation before."

"Well, I won't keep pressuring you, but you know how to find me when you get tired of using your finger to pleasure yourself."

"Wow, I see you hold nothing back."

"Never. It'll kill you if you let it."

I couldn't even respond. He was so bold about it that it was almost scary. The thing about it, though, his confidence was a turn-on. I didn't want to make a mistake and do something that I would regret but I could honestly admit since Black was away I'd needed sex, I'd yearned for it, but I held it together feeling like I had no other choice.

"I'll let you rest, if you need anything make sure you call me," he said as he got up and walked toward the door. I still sat there in shock. I didn't know what to do. The phone rang and startled me out of my stare.

"Hello?"

"Hey it's Trice, just called to see how you were."

"I'm okay, thanks for calling. How are things with you? If you need any money for Keshawn I'll have someone drop it off for you."

"I didn't call you for that. I actually believe we've grown to be friends and I wanted to check on you to see if you needed anything."

"No, I'm fine, I just want to come home but I can't bring the baby anytime soon so I'm a little sad about that."

"Aww, Keshawn is so excited; he wants to see her."

"Well, she'll be out of here soon enough. I have to stay for two more days then I'm going to stay at my dad's for a week or two before I go home."

"That's good. Well, I will call you again later to check on you, I just wanted to see how you were."

"Okay thanks a lot." I said before hanging up.

Immediately my mind drifted back to Money and what he'd said. I still didn't know what I planned to do but either way I had to do something because he wasn't going to give up until I either went through with it or I made it clear that I wanted nothing to do with him. Option two I wasn't so sure of. There was a part of me, the old me, the part that loved danger and attention. I still got a high from doing what I knew I had no business doing and resisting was one of the hardest things I'd ever have to do.

Two days later I was packed and ready to leave the hospital. I sat and held Dior for an hour before I left. My father had come to pick me up and take me over to their house. I wasn't too excited about it but I knew that I needed all of the help that I could get. I was surprised when I was wheeled out to the car and Javan was there as well. I knew that it was him because he looked exactly like my father. He was standing on the side of the car leaning up against it, looking around when he noticed me.

"Wow, you do look like Mom," he said, walking over and bending down to hug me.

"I'm so glad you came, this is such a surprise."

"Yeah, I'm sorry about the accident. I didn't want us to meet up this way but now that we have no choice we'll make the best of it." He laughed as he helped me into the backseat.

"Well, look at it this way, now I have a lot of time to catch up with my family." I smiled. Now that Javan was going to be around I felt better about spending time over with them. He made it that much more interesting. We began the drive over and engaged in conversation on the way. Once we reached the house Javan and me sat in the living room and talked for what seemed like an eternity.

"So how's school?"

"School's great but enough about me, let's talk about you. What do you do? Where's your job?"

"I don't work, I have a lot of businesses that I inherited from my husband when he died."

"So you're like rich or something?" His eyes grew wide.

"Something like that," I laughed.

"That's great, I always hoped that you were doing good. Though we never met I felt close to you. Mom never stopped talking about you. I even had your baby picture in my wallet. I waited for the day that we'd get to sit down and talk like this."

"I'm sad that I never knew about you but I have the rest of my life to enjoy you now."

I learned so much more about him as well as my mother and father and their families. I couldn't wait to meet them. I was losing the anger more and more each day and gaining love. I didn't stay but a week before I went back home but in that week a new world opened up for me. I was getting back on my feet and I planned on making a lot of changes for the better.

Chapter 21

Diamond

Money on My Mind

I was headed up to the sixteenth floor of Hahnemann Hospital as I did every morning to go visit Dior. I could get around on crutches against the wishes of my doctors but I had to go. I wasn't the type to lie down and let other people take care of me. I'd always been able to get up and do whatever it was I had to do for myself no matter what condition I was in. I waited on the elevator and as I stood there I saw a familiar face. It was Deidra, Mica's cousin. I almost wanted to avoid her; in a way I felt guilty about what I did, but then when I thought about the reason I did it I didn't feel so bad. She caught a glimpse of me and walked over to where I was standing.

"Diamond, is that you?"

"Wow, Deidra? I thought that was you. How are you?"

"I'm good, I haven't seen you in so long. How have you been? I see you on crutches—what happened?"

"I was in a car accident, unfortunately, but I'm okay."

"You're all grown up now, last time I saw you, you were a teenager."

"I know, time flies."

"Yeah, I wish Mica was still here. I know she would have loved to see you."

I stood there quiet. I assumed that she didn't know what happened between her and me. Did she even know that she was still alive? I didn't know how to approach that question so I decided not to even mention it at all.

"Well, I don't want to hold you up, it was nice seeing you," she said in my moment of silence.

"You too," I quickly responded to avoid any suspicion. She waved and walked away. I pressed the elevator button and waited for the next one to come. I stayed for my normal one-hour visit before going home. I was surprised when Money's car was parked in front of the hospital rather than JB's. JB was supposed to pick me up and give me a ride home because my mom and dad were both working.

"Where's JB?"

"He had to take care of something so I offered to come pick you up."

"Why?"

"Because I wanted to, why are you making things so difficult? A nigga can't be nice to you, I see."

"I didn't say that a nigga can't be nice, but we both know that you are not just being nice. You have an ulterior motive."

"That's not completely true."

"Well, what part of it is true, then?"

"Well, of course I'm aiming for something but it's real. I'm not gaming you up, though, if that's what you think."

"Honestly, I do."

By this time we were in the car and heading the short ten-minute drive to my house. I was practically staring a hole in the side of his face. He hadn't even blinked. I didn't know what it was about him but I was definitely drawn to him and I knew that sooner or later the shield that I had up would crack. Right now, though, I had to focus on getting my health back.

"Well, what do you need? I'm here at your feet; your wish is my command, if that's what it takes."

"You're really serious, huh?"

"As a heart attack. I'm a pretty straightforward dude and I hate to keep repeating it, but your man Black ain't going to be around and you're going to need somebody to help you run those businesses. Who better than me?"

"So that's it? You just want to take his place with the business—it really has nothing to do with me?"

"You're misreading me, it has everything to do with you. I'm trying to be that strong nigga that you'll need when you come to your senses and see that this shit ain't a game. He's not coming home."

"Why are you so sure that he's not coming home?" I was beginning to get annoyed with him again. I wasn't giving up on Black until I knew that for fact. Even then I still wouldn't stop loving him. No one could take that away. It didn't matter how much game he spit or how much attention he gave he wasn't Black and he'd never be no matter how hard he tried.

"I'm sure of it because I know how that shit works. It's okay to have hope—don't get me wrong. Who wouldn't in your situation? That doesn't mean I'm going to sit in the background and not go for what I want. Yeah, I want his spot but it's his spot with you. It ain't all about the money. I got plenty of that."

I sat there still staring at him. I was so confused. My mind, heart, and body were all being pulled in different directions. Maybe what he was saying was the truth and Black would never be home. What the hell was I supposed to do, lose everything? Or find a strong man to take his place? Then I thought that this could all be too premature. I was known in the past to let my body run my decisions but would it be the worst thing to give him a chance?

"I hear you, but you have to understand that until that's a proven fact I'm not going to just give up on him."

"And I don't expect you to."

"So what is it that you expect?"

"I expect you to let me in."

We were pulling up in front of the house at that moment and I felt that it was perfect timing. I wasn't ready to give him a decision. Once he parked I still sat silent. He looked over at me and didn't say anymore. He exited the car and walked around to the passenger side to help me get out.

"Thanks a lot for coming to get me."

"No problem, I can come in and help you out if you want me to." He smiled. He knew damn well I wasn't going to let him in.

"I'm fine, I can manage."

"I figured you'd say that but don't forget that I'm here," he said, walking back toward the car after I made it to the steps.

He got in his car and drove away. I made it inside and though he was gone he still lingered on my mind. I was trying extremely hard and it wasn't working. He'd made a mark and now that it was down it wasn't going to be easy to erase. Money, can't live with it, can't live without it. That statement was ringing louder than a school bell at eight A.M.

Chapter 22

Diamond

Two Temptations

Letters weren't enough and I still hadn't been able to see Black. I missed him desperately and I didn't know how long I could hold off. My knee was healed enough to get around without crutches. I'd gone back home and was doing pretty good. I was just on my way to head out to Gia's when the doorbell rang. I opened it to find Money standing there with flowers in hand.

"Wow, you're back to normal, I see. I wanted to come by and personally drop these off."

"You don't have to keep doing stuff like this, Money, you really don't."

"I know I don't have to but I want to. Is it all right if I come in?"

"Well, I was just on my way out, actually."

"Just for a minute, just long enough for you to put these in water." He passed me the flowers.

"Okay, I guess that's fine." I walked into the house, letting him in behind me. He followed me into the kitchen. I grabbed a vase from the cabinet and turned on the sink to fill it up as I took the flowers out of the plastic. "So how are things going at . . ." I hadn't even finished my sentence. I turned around and was met by a kiss. His lips were soft as cotton and they felt so good against mine that I couldn't resist. My mind was saying that this was wrong but my body was saying you need this. His arms had since wrapped around me and began caressing my back. It was sending chills through my body. You would have thought this was the first time that I'd been kissed. I was nervous about moving forward because I didn't know what would become of this. I wasn't ready to move on from Black but I was ready for the attention that Money wanted to give me. I closed my eyes and instead of fighting my body any longer I gave in and relaxed. He continued to kiss me intensely. His thick tongue was massaging mine as his hands moved from my back to my hips then the front of the jeans that I'd be wearing for only a few more seconds. He'd unbuttoned them, pulled them off, and placed me on the kitchen counter all within one minute or less. His face was then buried in my pussy and his tongue was massaging my clit as it had done my tongue before. My legs were wrapped around his head as I leaned back with both hands on the counter, bracing my body.

I moaned continuously. I wasn't sure if it was because I was deprived for so long or if it just felt that damn good but I was so loud the neighbors could probably hear me through the walls. I grabbed hold of his head just as I was about to erupt.

"Oh, shit, I'm about to cum," I yelled as my body shook uncontrollably. If I'd wrapped my legs around his neck any tighter I might have smothered him. He kept up the pace and I continued to shake, I couldn't stop. I wanted him to keep going but I wasn't sure how much more I could take. I had never been one to run away from some good loving but this felt different and maybe because it was so wrong. He stood up and licked his lips as if he'd just got finished eating a good steak. I smiled for the first time since we'd begun. He stared at me without speaking. His eyes were piercing with a sort of unknown agenda, but it continued to turn me on. I was still sitting in the same position as he removed a condom from his pocket, dropped his pants, and put the condom on his large, stiff dick, which was pointing in my direction. He walked over to me, opened my legs wider, making the path he was going for more accessible. I let out a sigh as he entered me. I was tight as vise grips and I could tell that he was enjoying the feeling of my tight pussy being wrapped around him. He grabbed hold of my waist and used his grip as leverage to push harder and harder. I could feel the juices coming out of me a running down onto the counter beneath me.

"You like this shit?"

"I love it," I moaned.

"Tell me again."

"I love it."

"You love what?"

"I love this dick," I yelled. I was in heaven and I realized how much I'd been missing with each passing second. He continued to move seamlessly in and out of me, picking up speed. I could feel myself reaching yet another climax. When I reached the peak, he suddenly stopped. The throbbing of his dick against my G-spot finished the job for him. I bit my bottom lip as I trembled in his arms. He stared at me for a few seconds and then starting pounding all over again.

I was exhausted but it felt too good to give up now. I sat there moaning and taking every inch it for the next twenty minutes when he finally let go of me and pulled away, giving me the same silent stare that he'd given me before he moved in on me.

"The bathroom is at the top of the stairs to the left."

He didn't respond but walked away and headed up the steps. I didn't get it but I wasn't going to worry myself trying to figure it out. Money was definitely different than any of the other men that I dealt with in the past. Here he went from talking all of the game in the world to silence. I got down off the counter and began to clean it off when I heard him coming back down the steps. I continued to clean, waiting for him to come back into the kitchen. I heard his footsteps and then I heard the front door open and close. Did he just walk out of here? What the hell was up with this dude? I went into the living room and called out his name. I didn't get an answer. I walked over to the window and peeked through the blinds. He'd gotten in his car and drove away. I felt used. I felt angry. I also somehow felt like I deserved it. I shouldn't have let the temptations get the best of me. I don't know what the hell I was thinking and if Black found out he would be furious. I hurried up the stairs to the bathroom and into the shower. I needed to clear my body of any scent that he may have left behind. My mind was wandering, I hadn't seen the baby and now I felt guilty about what just went down. Maybe going up to the hospital would make me feel better than I did now. I went out to the car and was just about to get in when his car sped around the corner and stopped next to mine. He jumped out of the driver's side, walked over to me and kissed me. He held on to my waist and stared into my eyes. I was too caught off guard to react. I wanted to slap him and yell for the way that he left out with not even a good-bye. Instead I let go of the tension in my body and enjoyed the kiss. He backed away with a devilish grin on his face.

"I'll be here tonight at nine, we're going on a date."

"What?" I threw my hands in the air I couldn't figure this guy out for the life of me.

He didn't respond, only smiling as he got back in his car and drove away. I didn't know what to say or think. I knew that I still felt used and that was something I wasn't used to dealing with. I drove down to the hospital and spent about an hour visiting before I went to the mall to find something to wear. I didn't want to get too jazzy because if anyone saw us out together I could play it off as a meeting. I didn't need word getting back to Black for fear that I'd lose him. What the hell was I thinking? I had to think about the situation logically. Was Money really into me or was he just into what he could get from me? I was going to figure it out one way or the other and going out with him would be the perfect way to do that.

I was dressed and ready at nine. I was actually ready by eight because I needed to give myself time to get my nerves together. I didn't want to seem like a teenager on her first date nor did I want to seem like a detective so I had to calm myself down enough for this date to go off without a hitch. Nine o'clock came and went. It was almost ten and I was pissed. I should have known better by the way he acted earlier in the day. I was just on my way upstairs when I heard a horn beeping. I walked over to the window and pulled the curtain and saw his black Mercedes double-parked in the middle of the street. I grabbed my bag off of the sofa and walked out of the door. I wanted to give him a piece of my mind as soon as I got out of the door but then I figured that would just give him the impression that I was really interested in him. I was interested but not solely in him. I was more interested in finding out what the hell he was up to.

I walked around the front of the car and gave him a look that said it all. I wanted him to think that I was upset; maybe then it would be a little easier to break through this shield that he was obviously holding up. I got in the car where he still seemed unfazed by the attitude I was giving off. He was cocky, but I liked it. It was something about a man with so much confidence and a challenge was something that I would never turn down.

"Nine o'clock, huh?" I said as soon as I planted my ass in the seat.

"Had some shit to do first but I'm here now so don't bitch about it when you can make the best of it."

Who the hell did he think he was talking to? Obviously me, because I was the only one in the car but I wasn't about to go out like that. No matter who it was, no one would talk to me like shit and get away with it. "Excuse me?"

"You heard me right. It doesn't make sense to bitch about it if you are still here with me. If you were that pissed then you should have stayed in the house."

"Where the hell do you get off talking to me like that? I don't know what type of chicks you are used to dealing with but I'm not one of them."

"I know you're not one of them because if you were you

would have never seen me again after I fucked you. So obviously you're different. Now, let's just go out and have a good time and forget about it."

Wow, I was shocked. Even though he made the comment in the rudest possible way that he could, it was cute. I got the point and what that meant was that I was more than a piece of ass. Not that I needed confirmation of that but it sounded good coming out of his mouth. I didn't respond. I didn't feel the need to make it bigger than it was. We arrived down on Delaware Avenue at the Chart House. I wasn't really all that excited about the food I was more excited about finding out more about him. We walked into the restaurant and were seated immediately. Money sat down and was still pretty silent.

"So tell me something about yourself."

"Tell you what?"

"About you. I don't know anything about you and we're practically partners."

"There ain't much to tell or much that I want to tell."

"Why, why is everything so cold and secret with you?"

"Because that's just the way that I am, it's not intentional it's just the way that it is." He was still cold as he picked the menu off of the table and began flipping through the pages.

"Don't you think you should change it? Or do you want to be alone all of your life?" I was staring at him so hard you'd think I could see through him.

"Alone is cool, at least when you fuck up you can't blame nobody but you. I like it that way."

"You are a strange character, I don't think I've ever met anyone like you." It was becoming a joke, and I was really beginning to think he was a comedian.

"What's so funny?"

"You, you are really cracking me up. I find it hard to believe you could be like this all of the time."

"So what do you think, I'm being hard for you?"

"Yeah, I think that you probably are trying to avoid falling for me."

"What?" He burst into laughter at this point. "You have to be kidding me, I don't have to put on an act for that. This is me and this is the way that I have always been."

"Well, even the strongest glass can be broken so don't think that it's impossible."

The waiter came over and took our order. That was the first time he smiled besides when her burst into laughter a few minutes earlier. I guess that last statement made him think about what I was saying. After the waiter walked away, I went right back in.

"When's the last time you've been in a relationship?"

"I'm in one now."

"Oh, really? So why are you here with me?"

"Beause I want to be, it doesn't have anything to do with that. Shit, you have a man, so why are you here with me?"

"Beause I want to." I laughed.

"Alright then, that makes us even."

"I guess you're right."

The rest of the night went much better than it began. After dinner we went over to my house where we ended the night with mind-blowing sex and this time a hug good-bye. Maybe I was breaking through that shell and would get some of the information that I needed. I knew that there was something that he was trying to get from me and though at first I gave in to temptation and had sex with him, I was now on the hunt and Money was the prey.

Chapter 23

Diamond

What am I Missing?

"I'm on my way, just be ready when I get there. I have something special planned," Money yelled over the loud music playing on his car radio.

"Okay, I'll be waiting at the door," I replied with a huge smile on my face.

"All right."

Click!

This thing was turning into something much more than I'd expected. I was actually beginning to enjoy his company. I still missed Black and I hated the fact that I couldn't see him but the letters that he'd send me were comforting. They made me feel like there was still hope for us. I hadn't accepted the fact that he was in jail waiting on a murder trial for something that I did but I knew that I was going to get him out of there some way, somehow. I was beginning to trust Money and I wanted to see how or if he could help me get Black off. I didn't know how to approach the subject since we'd been seeing each other so much. He pulled up in front of the house and beeped the horn as usual. I still hadn't gotten him to break that habit. I hurried out to the car, excited about what he had planned.

"So what is it that you have planned that's so special?"

"It won't be a surprise if I tell you. Don't worry, you deserve it."

"Okay," I said smiling. I was a sucker for surprises.

"So I got a letter from Black today and he wanted me to ask you if you'd help me with getting him out of jail."

"How the hell am I supposed to do that?" He seemed annoyed.

"Well, there's this chick named Mica who's pointing the finger at him. She's the only witness they have. Without her, they'll have to let him go. She's in the witness-protection program so we haven't been able to locate her. He said with your resources, you'd probably be able to."

He turned to look at me with a serious look on his face, "With my resources? What the hell does he mean by that?"

"Hell if I know, but that's what he said in the letter."

"Well, I'll see what I can do but I can't promise anything."

"Okay."

I wasn't sure where we were going but after that question the air in the car felt different. It had suddenly gone cold again like the first night that we were together. I felt like an ass for even bringing it up.

"So where are we headed?"

"You'll see," he quickly responded.

I sat back and kept quiet the rest of the ride. We arrived at a house in the Mount Airy section of the city. It was a pretty large house as all of the houses around it were. I felt special. I was finally going to see where he lived. I was glad that I had my gun with me, though. I remembered that he said he was in a relationship and I wasn't about to have his girl bust up in there acting a fool and not be able to protect myself. All of the lights were off inside the house but there were two other cars parked in the driveway, a blue Toyota and a black Mazda.

"Whose cars are these?" I asked as soon as I shut the car door behind me.

"Mine."

We walked up to the large wooden door quietly. I still wanted to know what the hell was going to happen that was so special that he couldn't tell me but I figured I could wait a little while longer if I waited this long. The house was huge inside but was so dark I stood still for fear that I would walk into something.

"Why are you standing there like a statue?"

"Because it's dark as . . ."

Just then the light came on. I laughed instead of finishing the sentence that I had started. He walked over to the radio and turned it on. The sounds of Raheem Devaughn, one of my favorite neo-soul singers, filled the room.

"This is a very nice place, you live here alone?"

"Why are you always giving me a survey? Just chill and have a seat. Your surprise will be here very soon."

I stared at him and his smile. He was so damn sexy it should be a sin. His hair was always perfect and he always smelled like Jean Paul Gautier cologne. His body was nice too. It wasn't as sculpted as Black's but it was pretty much running neck and neck. It was almost mouthwatering. I wanted to jump on him and get busy right then and there but I had to play his game. I walked over to the sofa and sat down. Crossing my legs, I began to shake my legs as if I was waiting impatiently.

"You crack me up, I'll be right back," he said laughing and heading out of the living room.

I sat there quiet, waiting for him to get back. I'd occasionally pick with my fingernails or run my fingers through my hair. I was bored as hell so the time seemed to be moving in slow motion. I heard his footsteps coming back toward the living room behind me. Out of nowhere I felt a hard hit on the back of my head. I tried to get up but my head was spinning. I fell back down in the chair.

"Hurry up and tie her up."

"I am hurrying, shit, stop rushing me, she's here now right where we wanted her."

I tried to open my eyes; my head was hurting like hell. When I was finally able to open my eyes I couldn't move my arms, they were tied behind my head. What the hell was going on? I tried to focus. There were two people standing in front of me, Money and Mica. What the fuck?

"What the hell is going on?"

"This is your surprise."

"What?"

"You really thought you could shoot me and get away with it? I knew you were cocky, but come on. You should have been more careful, now you're going to die and your boyfriend is going to spend the rest of his life in jail while we run his business."

"What do you mean we?"

"Oh, you still don't get it? Money is my man, I'm sure he told you that he had a woman, right? But that never stopped you before."

"It never stopped you either!" I yelled while trying to get my hands free.

"You're in no position to talk, remember that? I thought it would be good to watch you squirm like you watched me that day in the warehouse."

"I was the one that talked him into letting you go, so how can you compare that to this?"

"I'm not comparing it to that, I just thought that it would bring back memories. It's definitely bringing them back for me."

"What the hell do you want from me?" I yelled. I was getting angrier by the second. Mica wasn't the rough type so I knew she wasn't going to kill me.

"I want to watch you suffer and then I'm going to kill you. It's a shame your little baby is going to be parentless."

"Fuck you Mica, don't even talk about her. You're not going to kill me and you know it. You can try all that thug shit if you want. It won't work, because you of all people don't scare me."

"I'm cracking up over here. You probably thought my man really wanted you, huh? How does it feel to get played?"

"He did want me."

"Don't fool yourself, okay, he just talked a good game to bring you here today."

"That's what he told you?"

"That's what I know."

"Yeah, well, don't fool yourself because your man's been fucking me for weeks."

"Wow, you are a comedian." She laughed. I knew that I was getting under her skin.

"I'm dead serious and you're in denial. He's lying to you, sweetie, he just fucked me yesterday, as a matter of fact."

"Bitch, stop lying!" she yelled as she ran over to where I was seated and slapped me across the face. I laughed hysterically, which pissed her off even more. I was getting to her when her plan was to get to me. She'd never watch me squirm. I'd die before I'd give her that satisfaction.

"What are you doing, Mica? Calm down," Money yelled and grabbed her by the arm.

"What am I doing, what is this I hear about you fucking her? Is that true, Money?"

He turned and looked at me and then back at her, "No, she's lying," he said.

"I'm lying? So now I'm lying? You didn't say that shit when your face was buried in my pussy!" I yelled.

"You bitch," she yelled and tried to get back over to me but Money stopped her in her tracks.

"Look now, calm down, I didn't fuck her, okay. That bitch is lying. Now we have some shit to handle and Deidra is pulling up outside."

"I'm done with you, bitch, you better believe that shit," she yelled as she headed toward the door. Money was still standing there staring at me as if he wanted to tell me how sorry he was. "Let's go, Money, now!"

He followed behind her and walked out of the door. Soon I heard footsteps walking toward me and then Deidra appeared.

"Oh, my god, Deidra, I'm so glad to see you. Could you get me out of here?"

"I can't do that, baby girl."

"Why not, I though we were cool? You always told me that I was your little sister. What happened to that?" I pleaded.

"What happened? You tried to kill my flesh and blood. All of that shit went out the window the moment you shot her."

"It wasn't like that, Deidra. I never meant to hurt her, honestly. I was trying to kill Kemp and she just got caught in the crossfire. I didn't intentionally shoot her." I lied, hoping that I could get her to let me go.

"I wish that was true, Diamond, I really do."

"Well, what are you going to do? Be Mica's little flunky? I thought you were the older one here?"

"I'm not anyone's flunky and you know that. You can say what you want but pissing me off is not going to get me to let you go."

I sat there quiet for a few seconds. She was right; it wasn't going to work, so I had to figure something else out. I had to get her to let me go before Mica and Money returned.

"I'm sorry okay, I'm losing my mind here I need to get back to my baby."

"Baby? What baby?"

"I have a little baby, her name is Dior. She was premature so she's still in the hospital. Remember I saw you that day at the hospital? I was visiting her."

"I didn't know that, she never told me you had a baby."

"I do and I need to be there for her, you have to help me, Deidra. Black's already in prison for the murder and as-sault—why isn't that enough? My daughter is going to suffer for this."

Deidra sat there as if she was debating what her next move should be. I could see that I was getting to her heart and that was where I needed to be. Though it was the truth I was laying it on thick and it seemed to be working. Deidra had always been a good person and I didn't see that changing. I could always talk to her and though Mica and me were close, my relationship with Deidra felt more real. I felt like we were family and she treated me as if I were really related to her. She would also do what she had to do to protect her blood so I could see how Mica would use that to her advantage.

"Are you going to help me?"

She looked at me for a minute or two but still remained silent. She got up from the chair and paced back and forth, looking at me every few seconds. I continued to beg her to let me go and as she continued to pace the room. I knew that I was most likely running out of time the longer this went on. I had no idea what time they were coming back but I knew it would probably be pretty soon.

"I'm going to help you," she finally responded.

I smiled and began to work in my head what I was going to do to get out of here. She went to look out of the window before coming back to the chair where I was sitting. She untied me and gave me the keys to her car.

"You have to tie me up, this can't look like I willingly let you go." She grabbed hold of my arm.

I looked in her eyes and saw fear. Though I wanted to get out of there as fast as I could I had to do it. I couldn't let her take the heat for having the heart to let me go. I agreed and as she sat in the chair I tied her up. I hugged her before grabbing my purse from the table and running toward the door. Just as I was turning the knob I heard a car pulling up—it was them. What the hell was I going to do now? I ran back into the room and looked around like I was trying to find somewhere to hide. There didn't seem to be a back door that I could run out of either. I noticed a closet under the stairs. I ran over to it and hid inside. I heard them come into the living room where Deidra was sitting tied up in the chair. The door on the closet was wood and had slightly opened panels, sort of like a mini-blind. I could see out but you couldn't see in. I sat there quietly.

"What the hell?" Mica yelled, running over to Deidra. Deidra had her head down and picked it up just as she got down on her knees and touched her own leg.

"She got away, I'm sorry Mica she got away."

"How the fuck did that happen? Did you untie her?" Money yelled. I could hear the anger in his voice as he paced back and forth. "Damn, Mica, I told you we shouldn't have left her here alone."

Mica was untying Deidra while Money was looking out the window, probably trying to see if I was outside.

"I'm sorry, Mica, she tricked me into letting her loose, then she overpowered me."

"Deidra, this is all messed up what the hell are we going to do now?"

Money continued to pace the floor. He now had retrieved his gun from the small of his back and was waving it around in the air. "I'm going to kill her, I'm going to fucking kill her."

I thought that was the plan anyway. Maybe they weren't going to kill me and were only threatening me to see what I'd give up. I still didn't know how I was going to manage getting out of the house but I stood quietly in the closet, barely breathing. Even if that wasn't the plan in the beginning it was definitely the plan now.

Deidra was sitting in the chair crying what seemed to be

real tears. I prayed that she wouldn't have a change of heart and rat me out. "I didn't mean to cause any trouble Mica, I really didn't. She was just going to use the bathroom and . . ."

"Don't worry about it, Deidra, I know you didn't mean to. We'll take care of it, okay." Mica helped Deidra up to her feet.

"You're damn right we'll take care of it. Come on, let's get out of here and go find her." Money walked toward the door and motioned with his hand for them to follow. I waited until I heard the sound of the cars pulling out of the driveway before I came out of the closet. I slowly opened the door and walked out into the living room. I pulled my cell phone out of my bag and dialed JB.

"Hello?"

"JB, it's Diamond. I need your help, where are you?"

"I'm at the office, what's up?"

"Money tried to kill me, him and Mica."

"What? Where are you?"

"I'm going to come to you, I can't risk them coming back and finding me."

"Okay, well, meet me at the office."

"I don't want to do that either, I'm afraid he's going to come there looking for me. Meet me at the warehouse. I'll get a cab to bring me there."

"Cool, I'll be there."

I hung up and ran out of the front door. I walked for blocks until I saw a cab riding by unoccupied and flagged it down. I sat low in the seat just in case they happened to drive by. We made it to the warehouse about twenty minutes after the cab picked me up. I jumped out of the car and paid the fare. JB was standing outside of the door when I got there.

"What the hell happened?"

"Money drove me to this house where they hit me over the head and tied me up. I thought they were going to kill me."

"Why were you with him in the first place? I told you I didn't trust him."

"I thought he was a good dude but it was all a setup—everything from the beginning. From the moment he met you and got close to Black it was all in their plan."

"What plan?"

"They wanted Black to go to jail then they were going to kill me and take over everything that we have."

"I should have known that muthafucker was up to something. I didn't see how shiesty this nigga really was. Damn, this shit is all my fault."

"It's not your fault. You didn't know."

"Black's not going to see it that way. I'm the one that brought him to his attention."

"Damn," he yelled. He was angry and rightfully so. I think that he was more angry at himself than he actually was at Money.

"We have to get rid of them, if not they won't stop and Black will end up in jail for the rest of his life. We can't let that happen, JB."

JB sat there staring into his hands as if he was trying to come up with a plan in his head. I hoped that he'd come up with a plan because I couldn't think of anything to do to take care of them. I needed his help and I prayed that he would come through for Black and me. I shouldn't have been so fast to jump in bed with Money. I should have listened to my heart and not let the lust win. Maybe then I would have been

able to see through the facade and been able to protect myself. They could have killed me and left my baby an orphan.
It was time that I started being smarter about what moves I
made. I had to be certain that I didn't miss anything anymore
that could potentially have such a devastating effect on my
life. Especially now that my life wasn't just my own.

JB assured me that he'd get Money by acting as if he didn't
know anything about what happened with me. He wanted me
to hide out and he'd have everyone out in the streets looking
for me, including Money. We still had to figure out how to get
to Mica. Now that I knew where she stayed it shouldn't be as
hard as it was before. I went out of state to a house Black and
I owned by the shore. I planned to stay there for a few weeks
until things blew over back in Philly. I arrived at the house
and everything was covered in white sheets just the way we'd
left them. I hadn't been there in months and every sheet was
covered with dust. I took a deep breath and I stepped inside. I
felt like for once I could rest. I went in my bag and pulled out
a photo of Dior. I told the hospital that I would be gone for a
few weeks but I'd call everyday. I said that there was a family
emergency so that they wouldn't report me to child services.

After I cleaned up a bit I sat down on the sofa and lay my
head back. I closed my eyes and thanked God that I was still
here. He'd given me another chance and I wasn't going to take
it for granted any longer. I curled up with a blanket and the
photo and tried to fall asleep.

Chapter 24

Diamond

One Last Breath

The ringing on the phone was extremely loud. I attributed that to the fact that it was so quiet in the house. I was losing my mind and I couldn't wait to get back to my life, civilization, as I called it. I rolled out of bed and grabbed the phone off the nightstand.

"Hello?"

"It's done, you can come back now."

"What's done, JB?"

"Money, I took care of him."

"What about Mica?"

"I need your help for that, I need you to show me where she is."

"I can tell you, JB, I'd really rather stay away until everything is taken care of."

"I need your help, Diamond."

I sat quiet for a minute. Hearing that Money was dead and gone was like music to my ears. I felt like there was a weight lifted off my shoulders but I knew it wasn't over. It couldn't be over until Mica was with him. There was no way we could get Black out of jail with her still alive.

"Okay, I'm coming home. I'll be there later on today."

"Call me when you're back in town, we can get busy as soon as you're here."

"Okay."

I hung up the phone and looked around the room. I wasn't sure if I was ready to face her again. I hadn't done such a good job the first time I tried to kill her. I kept thinking back to that night and how she managed to slip away. I kept blaming myself for all of the trouble that Black was going through. I blamed myself for everything. I hadn't been able to do one thing right with my life. From the outside looking in it seemed that I had everything and that I was always lucky. But my life was in shambles. I was never happy regardless of how much money I had and it took me this long to figure it out. It took me to almost lose everything to appreciate the one thing that I always had. I always had life and I'd always had good sense, I just chose not to use it.

I gathered up my things and packed them in the car. I was on my way back to Philly and back to snatch my life back. Once I got back home I called JB as he'd instructed. He came over to the house immediately. I heard the knock at the door and hurried to go answer it.

"Hey, come in, I just have to grab a couple of things." I walked away from the door after I answered it. JB followed me into the house after closing the door behind him.

"So that was pretty quick, I didn't expect you to get home so fast."

"Well, I want to get this over with, I need to see my man walk out of that prison."

"That's not going to happen."

"What do you mean . . ." I turned around to find JB standing there pointing a gun at me. What the hell was going on? "What's going on, JB?"

"I'm sorry you got caught up in this, Diamond, but this is the way that it has to be."

"What do you mean?"

"I mean, I wish that I could keep you alive but I know you'll never go along with this. I thought that we could be together but then you started fucking Money. Why did you go and do that, Diamond?"

"How did you know about that?" Tears started to form in my eyes. I never expected JB to be the one out to get me.

"He told me. We were working together to get rid of Black; you were supposed to be with me but you went and fucked him like a whore." He was yelling and waving the gun around. I was standing still, crying.

"Please, JB, don't do this, we can be together, we just have to go get rid of Mica, remember."

"That bitch is already dead. I took care of her and her man."

"How are you going to get what you want without me? Black is going to get out of prison now that she's dead."

He stared at me. He hadn't thought that far. He'd killed the only witness keeping Black in jail so unless he planned on killing him too his plan would never work.

"Fuck Black," he yelled. "You think I'm scared of him, I will kill that muthafucker so fast."

"I didn't say you were scared of him, I said that we can be together. You and me can do this." I was trying to get his confidence. I was still crying but I was trying to mask it, but it wasn't working out like I thought it would.

"Do you think I'm stupid? You actually think you can fool me? I'm not an asshole, Diamond. I know that you're only saying this so I can let you go."

"I mean it, I mean every word, JB. We can be together."

"I don't want you now, I know that you're a fucking whore. You cheated on Black with Money and Black hadn't even done shit to you. I know your kind and there's no way this shit would work now."

"Yes, it can work, you just have to give it a chance." I moved close to him and tried to win him over by looking in his eyes. He wouldn't look at me, only backing away the closer that I got. "Please give us a chance."

I saw a shadow behind him but I didn't want to focus on it. That shadow turned out to be Tommy. He put his finger up to his mouth as to say be quiet. JB was starting to warm up to me. I could tell because he wasn't backing away any longer.

"I'm sorry for what I did, I didn't know that you wanted to be with me."

"You're not sorry, you were willing to throw it all away for some dick," he began to yell again.

"I am sorry, I wish that it was you."

He turned to look at me again. Just then Tommy's shoes made a sound. JB turned around with his gun drawn. Tommy shot him twice before he had a chance to shoot back. I dropped down to the ground and burst into a hysterical cry. Tommy walked over to me and pulled me up from the floor. I grabbed hold of him and continued to cry. He walked me over to the couch where I sat down. He dialed the police on the house phone and reported the shooting.

"What are you doing, Tommy, you're going to go to jail!" I tried to grab the phone out of his hand.

"Look, take this gun. You're going to say that you shot him after he burst into your house and tried to attack you. Everything will be fine, I promise."

I'd heard that line too many times in the past few weeks. For once I wanted to believe it. I shook my head and agreed to tell the story to the police. The sirens and red and blue lights were flashing within ten minutes. The cops ran in with their guns drawn. I was still sitting on the sofa with the gun in my hand. Tommy had left out of the back door before they'd arrived.

"Ma'am, are you hurt?"

"No, I'm not hurt."

"Drop the gun, please."

I obeyed. I sat the gun down on the floor. The officer ran over and kicked the gun over. Another officer reached down to check JB's pulse and looked up, shaking his head, confirming that he had no pulse. I was in a daze. I still wasn't grasping what had happened. The cops left me on the sofa while they began marking the scene. I was taken down to the police station where I gave them the story of what happened at the house. I stayed for a few hours before they released me. I couldn't even sleep when I got home. I got up in the middle of the night and went over to Kiki's house.

Instead of giving me words of wisdom, she gave me comfort. I fell asleep in her bed finally after an hour or so. She lay next to me holding my hand. The day had been such a traumatic day and I still didn't know what was to come. I was still afraid. I didn't know who to trust. The person that Black trusted the least had been the one to save my life. Everything was so out of control. At that point, I didn't know if they could ever be the same.

Chapter 25

Black

Home Sweet Home

Finally, I was going home. I told Ms. Baker not to tell Diamond, I wanted to keep it a surprise. I hadn't seen her since the day that they dragged me out of the courtroom. I never wanted her to run up here and see me in this cage nor did I want my child witnessing that. I wasn't allowed visitors and letters still hadn't been enough. I missed her and I wanted to get home to feel her again. I'd heard how things were on the streets and I couldn't believe how JB turned on me. Jealousy and envy will make people do some strange things and that was definitely true with that situation.

What went wrong? Niggas were trying to kill me, my girl, and take my spot. When this shit first started JB was the main one, saying that he had my back no matter what happened and it turned out that he had more than my back in mind. I would have never thought that he'd turn on me. I would have thought Tommy would have been the one. When the Kemp shit started he was sure that Kemp wasn't alive. I guess it made sense now that he had so much confidence because he knew damn well he wasn't alive. He knew because it was him and that nigga Money all the time. Tommy made it his business to get word to me and I owed it to him for saving Diamond's life.

Tommy picked me up from the bus where they'd left me. I looked like shit and there wasn't any way I was going to show my face to her looking the way that I did. Tommy got out of the car and walked over to me. I stuck my hand out to shake his. Instead of shaking my hand he hugged me, which caught me completely off guard.

"It's good to see you, man."

"Thanks so much for all that you've done."

"No problem, man, I told you I was here for you.

"I need you to do me a favor before you take me home. I need to get a haircut and get some gear. I can't go home like this."

"Already got that shit lined up, got some jeans and shit in the back for you. Nigga, I know you too well." He laughed.

"My man, thanks!" I gave him dap.

We drove down to the barbershop where I got a fresh haircut, then he drove me over to his house so I could shower. I felt like new money when I got out of there. I was ready to go home. We pulled up in front of the house and I was more nervous then I'd ever been. I felt like I was going on a job interview or some shit. I didn't know what to say to her. I hoped that it would come natural. Tommy pulled out as I made it up to the door. I knocked lightly. It was strange knocking on my own door but I almost felt like a stranger visiting for the first time.

"Coming," she yelled as she neared the door. My heart was pounding a mile a minute. I couldn't wait to see her face. She opened the door and stood still as a statue. Tears came out of her eyes before she moved out of the door to wrap her arms around me. "How did you get out? Why didn't they tell me?" She cried and smiled at the same time.

"I wanted to surprise you, I missed the hell out of you." I grabbed hold of the sides of her face to bring her into a kiss. I wanted to make love to her at that moment and I would have if I could.

"The baby's inside, come on in so you can see her."

We walked into the house. I dropped my bag near the door and followed her upstairs toward the baby's room. She was asleep but as beautiful as a porcelain doll. I didn't want to wake her so I didn't reach in to pick her up. I just stood there looking at her, then looking at Diamond.

"Why are you looking at me like that?"

"Because I never would have imagined you being a mother. I'm sorry I couldn't be there for you."

"It doesn't matter, you're here now and everything is going to be okay."

I believed it. I was focused and there wasn't anything that was going to mess this up. We'd come too far for that. I pulled her out of the room and into the bedroom. I couldn't wait another minute to touch her. She smiled as I moved closer to grab hold of her. She helped me by taking off her clothes. I stared at her body and it was perfect, just as I'd left it. I'd heard about her and Money but I didn't care. I knew that everything she did was to get me out of jail and I couldn't let that affect me.

She lay on top of the bed as I undressed. I wasn't even fully naked before I opened her legs, got on my knees, and met her

clit with my lips. It was as sweet as honey and I was savoring
every drop. She was moaning as I continued to fuck her with
my tongue. She used her hips to grind harder against it. I
stuck two fingers inside of her pussy as I used my other hand
to slide my boxers off. My dick was as hard as a brick and after
months of jacking off I could finally feel her wrapped around
it.

I got up from the floor and slid my dick inside of her. She
gasped for air as if she wasn't expecting it. I pulled her legs up
around my neck and fucked her like a racehorse for the next
half hour. I erupted all inside of her and fell down on her like
I'd lost every bit of my energy right along with the cum that
was now running out of her.

She got up from under me and headed to the bathroom. I
was still laying across the bed when she turned on the shower.
For once I felt like I didn't want to hurry out of the house. I
wasn't thinking about work but instead I was thinking about
her. I got up off of the bed and jumped in the shower with
her.

"You really do miss me, huh?" She giggled just before facing me then going down to her knees and taking my dick into
her warm mouth. I grabbed onto the side of the wall and let
out a sigh similar to the one that she'd let out earlier. Her lips
wrapped around my dick with the water pouring all over her
turned me on more than I'd ever been with her. It wasn't long
before I bent her over and fucked her for another fifteen minutes. Finally, I allowed her to shower. She kissed me before
leaving me in there alone. I washed up before jumping out
and getting dressed again. She was downstairs in the kitchen
making the baby a bottle.

"Trice is on her way over, I called her."

"What? Why would you call her?"

"Because your son wants to see you and Trice is cool. There won't be any drama, trust me."

"Since when have you two become friends? I see I've missed a lot more than I thought I did. I would have never imagined that."

"Right after you went in, she came to me and let me know that she needed some help. I wasn't going to turn her away, so I helped her and we've been cool ever since."

"You should have told me she was coming. I have to run out and meet Tommy back at the warehouse," I lied. I wasn't really ready to be in the same house with both of them. I thought of it as being a very uncomfortable situation.

"Babe, you just got home. Just see him and then you can go."

Damn, I was going to have to deal with it sooner or later so I thought, fuck it, I might as well get it over with. It wasn't long before she was ringing the bell. I opened the door and my son ran right to me, hugging my legs. Trice smiled and gave me a quick hug.

"Good to see you, he missed you a lot," she said, walking into the house. Diamond had come out of the kitchen and was standing in the hall.

"I have to run, but I'm going to spend a lot of time with him this week, I promise. I just have to go take care of some things right now. I didn't know that you were coming until a few minutes ago."

She looked disappointed. I wasn't trying to upset anyone but I really did have some shit to handle. I needed to get back to the office to begin rebuilding.

"It's cool, I know you have to go work. We'll hang out here for a little while but I'm going to hold you to that. He needs to be with you."

"And he will be."

I hugged him again and kissed Diamond before I left out of the house. It actually wasn't as bad as I thought it would be. I grabbed my keys off the key rack and hopped into the car. I was on my way down to the office. I had so much on my mind. There was so much to do and now that Money, Mica, and JB were gone, there wasn't anything to worry about. Everything should be smooth sailing from that point on. I was back at home where I needed to be and the sweet smell of success was flowing up my nose as I drove up the expressway with the windows down. A change was coming and I was going to embrace it.

Chapter 26

Diamond

Trust

I was worried that Black would find out about Money and me. I enjoyed making love to him every night since he came home but it wasn't the same. It was almost as if he knew but didn't want to tell me. I wanted to just lay it out on the table but that most likely wasn't the right thing to do. He hadn't said anything about marrying me either. Maybe he changed his mind and decided that I wasn't marriage material. I was driving myself crazy worrying about it. I felt like I had to come clean so that we could move on. I would have to accept whatever was thrown my way afterward but I couldn't keep it inside any longer. He came home and I was sitting in the living room with the lights on but nothing else was on.

"What's wrong?" He could always tell when I was upset. I was beating myself up all day and I was probably about to make a huge mistake.

"There's something that I have to tell you. I have to be honest and I can't move forward without telling you." I could feel the tears forming in my eyes; it was going to kill me to hurt him but I didn't see what other choice I had.

"Look, Diamond, I just got back. There's no need to go into all of that. Let's enjoy this time that we have together."

"No, I have to tell you and I have to tell you now." I was determined to get things off of my chest.

"If it's about Money and you, I already know and I don't care."

I looked up at him, stunned. I wasn't sure if I'd heard him right.

"You don't care?"

"No, I don't care and I want to forget about it."

"But how can we have trust after that?"

"Diamond, I trust you and I'm not questioning you about it because I understand how that could have happened. I love you and I'm going to marry you. I don't care what happened when I wasn't here. I'm worried about what happens from this point on."

Was he serious? I've never found a man who could trust a woman after they'd cheated. I mean, I dealt with him even after I knew about all the women he chose to sleep with but that was different. That's what I thought I was supposed to do.

"Are you really going to marry me?"

"I just said I was, why do you think I bought you that big-ass ring?" He laughed. He pulled me close to him. "Look, I'm not perfect and I know that I've done some things in the past. I'm not going to leave you for doing the same shit that I did. We are going to start fresh from this point on. Fuck the past."

"Sounds good to me," I laughed as I hugged him.

I was happy the way that things were turning out. They were actually going better than I could have imagined. I thought for sure once I told him about Money we would be over. Following that day things were good. Black and I planned to get married in the spring and things couldn't have been better. The business was going great and I had even talked Black into making Tommy a partner. Tommy was strong and he'd saved my life. I had to find a way to pay him back. What better way to say thank you than running a major drug empire?

I thought back to all of the things that I'd been through in my life. It was always good to reflect on your past to appreciate the things that you've learned along the way. We all make mistakes and every mistake teaches us something. Whether we learn from them or not is up to us. There were a lot of times that I did things that I swore I'd never do again only to end up doing them again. Maybe I was a hard learner but whatever the case I'd managed to look back and smile. I smile because I made it out alive and strong. Things could have gone a whole lot different if I would have let those mistakes get the best of me. There were people in my life who made such an impact. That night, I lay in bed thankful for my life and all that I had to look forward to. There had been a lot of bumps along the way and I'd still been able to succeed. There were times that I felt like I didn't deserve to be here, but now, I knew that I did. I'd done a lot of wrong in my life but maybe that was also a part of the plan that was lay out for me. I believe all of it was even down to my teenage years. I closed my eyes with Black nestled next to me and reminisced.

I thought about Johnny and how things could have been different for us. Maybe if I hadn't pushed so hard he wouldn't have spent the rest of his life in jail. At the time, I felt like no one should be abused the way their father abused them. I questioned if it was really my influence that caused him to pull the trigger. Maybe Mica and I wouldn't have fallen out either. At one time we were the best of friends, playing jump rope, doing each other's hair, and playing in her mother's makeup. I missed those times and was sad that one simple push would not only cause me to lose Johnny but her as well. She never forgave me, even though the day I walked in the warehouse and found her tied up, I saved her life. Kemp would have murdered her for sure if I hadn't talked him out of it. I felt that I owed her—I felt that once I saved her she'd forgive me for ruining her life. At fifteen, I couldn't possibly know what would happen to her family once her father was killed. She felt the brunt of her mother's depression and to this day hated me because of it. Yes, I shot her but I don't think even that angered her more that what happened with Johnny. We never got that friendship back because deep down I know that she never forgave me for what happened to him.

I thought about my mother and how I left her to fend for herself when I met Davey. I still believed that if I'd helped her get out of that neighborhood instead of only worrying about me maybe she would have still be alive. Drugs took control of her and there wasn't any turning back. What started as depression soon evolved to something much more after my father walked out on us. She leaned on the drugs as a crutch—the crutch that would later kill her. I missed her and I felt like I was cheated out of time with her. There could have been so much more to our relationship but we both let temptations on the outside keep us apart. I was lured by the money and she was lured by the drugs, two different things, but both highly addictive. I felt like I lost a part of me the day that I found out she was gone. I hadn't even had a chance to say good-bye or kiss her one last time. Drugs robbed me of telling her I loved her.

I thought about my Aunt Cicely and how evil she had been my entire life. I felt bad for the way I treated my grandmother because of things that she said or did to me. She couldn't control the things that she did and it took me this long to realize that. She was the only grandmother that I'd known and she was always there for me when other people weren't. I planned to make things better between us even though I was still angry that she didn't tell me about the funeral, I still didn't understand how they'd bury my mother and not think I needed to know. How anyone could be so cruel I'd never know. I knew that it wasn't all her doing and I put most of the blame on Cicely but she didn't try to reach out to me so that made her just as guilty. I still had to forgive and the situation with Black showed me that it was definitely possible.

I thought about Davey and how my life took a turn for the worse. I let him take advantage of me in ways that damaged me as a woman. I knew that I wouldn't have made a lot of choices in my life if it weren't for things that I allowed him to do to me. I loved him with all of my heart and he stomped on it every chance that he had. I was happy that I was finally able to move on and find love in myself.

Kiki, my best friend, had always been there for me regardless of the dumb decisions that I made. I was lucky to have her in my life and she'd always be an important factor. There wasn't any one like her and that's what made her special.

I thought of Kemp. He was one of the men that I didn't give a chance to show his full potential. I went into that relationship in a bad state of mind. Maybe he wasn't perfect but maybe things could have worked out differently had I given him the chance and loved him the way that he intended on loving me. I was sorry that I took him away from his family and his child. Now that I had my own child and faced death, I know how devastating that must have been. Maybe all of the things that I went through I deserved because of what I did and I've accepted that.

I thought about Money and how I fell right into his trap. How could I have been so stupid believing that he really wanted to be with me? I'd been a fool more times than I could count on my hands but I could admit that being with him was one of the biggest mistakes I made in my life.

Then there are my parents. I hated them for years because of what I assumed they should have done. Who's to say that my life would have been any better if they'd kept me after all? Javan turned out okay but things could have been different for both of us if I would have been there. Maybe leaving me was best and I'd finally come to that conclusion and stopped hating them. I was finally accepting the way things were and loving them for who they are and not the people that they were in the past.

Then there was Black, the man that I loved more than any man that I'd been with my entire life. I hadn't found a man that loved me the way that he did. When I met him I never would have thought that we would be where we were at that point. We had evolved into a relationship that I'd always drea-med I'd be in but never thought I'd see.

Dior, my beautiful baby girl who'd changed me from the moment she fluttered in my stomach. The old conniving Dia-mond was an object of the past and I'd matured into a woman and a mother. The path that I took to get where I am to-day was a long one and it was a rough one. Everyone that I'd encountered in my life had all added to the person that I've become. Looking back, if you'd ask me would I take any of it back and my answer would be no. I wouldn't change a thing because changing one thing in the past would alter the future and my future was with Black and Dior.

Chapter 27

Black

Our Way

"So how does it feel?" Tommy asked, raising his glass to mine.

"It feels good, man, it feels damn good." I laughed. We were out celebrating because business was back on track. Money was flowing in and the soldiers were all in line. I never thought I'd be enjoying this moment with Tommy. Thinking back, all I could think of was Kemp and how he promised me that I was destined for greatness. I used to feel bad about being with Diamond but now I didn't. I knew that this was the way that things were supposed to be. I remember sitting with Kemp when he made a million dollars. We were sitting in his living room and we had a bottle of champagne sitting on the table. We were both pretty drunk.

"A million muthafucking dollars, do you believe that shit, nigga?"

"I knew you'd do it, you always said that you would."

"I sure did and you're getting to enjoy it with me. Being on top is a wonderful thing and you'll be here one day."

"I feel you and I'm happy to witness this shit for real."

"I'm king of the world, nigga, ain't that what they say!" He was standing on top of the sofa with a glass in his hand.

"That's what they say." I was cracking up. This nigga was drunk as hell and spilling shit all over himself and me.

"On some real shit though," he said, sitting back down next to me. "When I'm dead and gone, you're the only nigga that I'd want to have this shit. Even down to my bitch, you can have it all. I mean that shit man, I love you like a brother."

"I love you like a brother too."

"Let's drink to that shit then," he yelled as he grabbed the bottle off the table and instead of pouring it he toasted my glass with it and drank the rest of it. I laughed that night but I believed that what he said was true. If there was anyone that he wanted to have all that he accomplished when he was gone, that person was me. I felt good knowing that he wouldn't have wanted it any other way.

Now, I had it all. Everything that was his, even his woman was mine. Tommy looked at me and began waving his hands in front of my face to break my stare.

"Yo', what the hell are you thinking about, man?" He laughed as I turned to look at him.

"I was just thinking about Kemp and something that he once said to me. He told me that I would have everything that was his when he was dead and gone."

"What the hell made you think about that?"

"Because I used to feel bad about being here and I felt like I didn't deserve it."

"Man, if anybody deserves it, you do. You deserve it all, even Diamond."

I looked at him and just nodded my head. At least there

was someone on this earth who felt the way that I did. I looked back on my life and the way that things had turned out. I was satisfied with that and I was looking my future in the eye ready to take it head-on. Now looking at Tommy and knowing what he'd done for me I could see how Kemp felt the way that he did back then. I lifted my glass and turned it in Tommy's, direction.

"In the words of Kemp, when I'm dead and gone there's no one that I'd want to have everything that's mine. Even my woman or bitch as he'd say," I laughed. "On some real shit, Tommy, that person is you. When I'm not here it's all yours and I mean that shit from the heart." He looked at me as if there was something that he wanted to say. I wasn't sure what the look was for but he sat silent for a minute or two before he raised his glass to mine, looked at me and said, "That's real shit, and I'll handle it with care!"

About the Author

Brittani Williams was born and raised in Philadelphia, PA, where she currently resides with her six year old son. She completed her first manuscript in 2005 which was titled *Daddy's Little Girl*. After months of research she found a publishing company that she wanted to submit to. She submitted the manuscript and received a quick response. The last two years have definitely been a blessing for Brittani with the release of *Daddy's Little Girl* and tons of great feedback from readers all over. She has had the opportunity to participate in two anthology projects *Fantasy* (Urban Lifestyle Press) and *Flexin' & Sexin'* (Life Changing Books) with some of the hottest authors in the game. With the release of *Sugar Walls*, her sophomore novel she had four projects in circulation, all released in the same year. In 2008 she returned even stronger with *The Cathouse*, a novel that she co-wrote with authors Anna J. and Laurinda D. Brown in June and *Black Diamond* 2008 with Urban Books. In 2010 the highly anticipated sequel to *Black Diamond 2: Nicety* will hit stores everywhere. In addition to writing, Brittani is also the owner of Ms. B graphics—her graphics design company which has been flourishing each day. She is currently working on her fifth and sixth novels and the stage play for *Black Diamond*. For more information on Brittani visit her online at www.BrittaniWilliams.com, www.myspace.com/msbgw or www.msbgraphix.net